I0723054

in case of emergency press

We are proud to acknowledge the Traditional Owners of
country throughout Australia and to recognise their
continuing connection to land, waters, and culture.
We pay our respects to their Elders.

We support recognition, reconciliation, and reparation.

Cherrystone Lane

David L Hume

in case of emergency press
https://icoe.com.au
Travancore, Victoria
Australia

Published by in case of emergency press 2024

Cover photo and title page image: **Daria Głodowska**, *Pixabay*
Photo of the author: **Meng Koach**

ISBN: 978-1-7637749-0-2

Dedication

This book is dedicated to those that came long after the land was stolen from the traditional owners: the Melukerdee people, and shaped the land as we see it today.

The orchardists that planted,
the pickers that harvested.
Those that came to stay,
those that came and went away.

Life is just a bowl of cherries
Don't take it serious; it's too mysterious

Life is just a bowl of cherries
— Lew Brown / Ray Henderson 1931

Table of Contents

Author's Note

With the exception of the first and last stories, I have crafted the other stories so that they may be read in any order. I encourage the reader to dip into them as you choose, thereby arranging your own collage of the mostly real setting and mostly fictitious people I have written.

Cherrystone Lane

David L Hume

Prologue

Cherrystone Lane

Cherrystone Lane is no more a lane than Temperance Lane, in the nearby town, is the address of God fearing tee total Congregationalists. No broken bottles or bones of drunks and other addicts of mind and mood altering substances set the latter's path. But Cherrystone Lane is built of stones pitted from fruit that sets on trees, lined up in rows, in yards and orchards planted long ago.

Along the rivulet of the same name, washed of poetics to a mundane creek by those lacking knowledge of local language, it is said and written into local legend that, over the span of man, Cherrystone Lane grew as a child does each year. Its history not marked by notches on doorjambs, but along the rivulet's course by stones and pips, graded and tamped for road base.

They spoke well of apricots, in 1936. Dried to chewy sweetness or pulped to nectar, thick and grainy then teamed with roosters surplus to hens. Most of all they celebrated the new cottages and community built along the new laid quarter mile.

Some years later they hailed the bounty of plums dried to prunes, forced on children and ailing elders for their propensity for regularity and again the quarter mile of new laid road, new laid gardens and orchard plots. There were apples too and while they gave health and brewed up wild and dried and stewed brought much needed wealth they built no road.

Today fields of cherries dominate, beneath stretched black veils, bird proof net, that carries its shade from Cherrystone Lane across the valley to Desecration Road, recently rebirthed in the light of the desecration of First Nations folk.

First world folk, as we are dubbed, are today strung along the Lane, as most residents call it, renovating ancient timber homes, converting pickers huts and packing sheds, grubbing out ancient trees once sculpted to wine glass fullness, constructing mansions on hills once out of reach. Staking driveways of silver birch, they generate new stories, new legends of Cherrystone Lane, not of pip and stone but imagined and set on the leaves to follow.

66 Cherrystone Lane

— today and tomorrow

Everything

'You really can see everything,' he says soon after he arrives. Usually I give him a cuppa, he takes off his backpack and we wander over to the big window. He sips at his coffee, finds it too hot, then makes his pronouncement. It's as if a sip of scalding milky coffee pings his eyes open like a much stronger stimulant. Today he finds his own way, empty handed, from the dull dark entry hall to the sunny window, with a view up and down and across the valley, that shrink his pupils to dots.

'Quite true,' I call from the kitchen, 'and what I can't see I make up.' He mouths the last part with me, silently.

'See that girl dawdling down the road,' I point to a sullen figure, hooded head down, shoulders hunched, dragging her feet. I splash warm milk into his coffee. 'She lives up the end, under the big pines, the last house. There's at least two other women in there, family, I think. I don't like the look of her.' I pass him his passable latte and we sit in the glare.

'Thanks,' he says, taking the cup by the handle, raising it to his lips before looking up. 'Geez who clocked you, old man?'

We sit in the window. He waits for an answer. 'It's nothing.' I feel the fading tenderness around my eye. A tenderness you don't feel, unless some fool reminds you about it.

'Looks like a real shiner,' he attempts to drink his coffee. It's too hot. 'So come on who smacked you?' he persists.

'It's nothing. Could have been anyone of a hundred.'

'Well, yeh,' he says slow and deliberately with a hint of sarcasm, 'you've pissed off hundreds, including those that live along the Lane,' he raises his coffee but doesn't drink goes on, 'and they're the only people you see now. You even get your groceries delivered now. You've nothing to pay for and I bring your other stuff.

'I have to get my groceries in from the road and that's all I need out there, thank you very much,' I lean back, cradling my unadulterated coffee, in mock hurt.

'Oh yeh, to the bottom of the drive for a couple of bags.' He snorts like a horse to dismiss my claim.

'I caught that girl eyeing up my shopping last week,' I tell him pointing through the glare at the dawdling figure. 'And what makes you think I've upset everyone along the road. Some I haven't even met.' I finish, adopting a snooty tone.

He gestures to the other end of the long sunny window where my paintings and sketches rest stacked and on easels and chairs waiting to go on the wall. 'You turn everyone into clowns, and no one likes being made into a fool.'

'I do no such thing,' I grump back. 'I use their likeness, their actions, their being to make pictures.'

'Pictures that take the piss.'

'Pictures of ordinary folk. If anything, I make them less ordinary. Caricatures,' I don't want to argue so take a breath. 'Besides, they don't know anything about art, go to galleries or look at paintings. So how would they know.'

'They read the local paper and the paper thinks you're some kind of once famous artist.'

'Once,' I spit, indignantly, then let it go. He's right, I've had my day.'

'And you should never have put your work in the town hall exhibition.'

'It's good work, I can still make good pictures. Besides, I sold a lot.'

'Yeh,' he snorts like a horse again, 'to tourists that want to connect with the countryside and see bizarre bumpkins, doing bizarre bumpkin things as some sort of bizarre representation of the countryside. Put it this way you're never going to win the people's prize.'

I have to agree with his last point, so say nothing.

He changes the subject, 'You know I can take you shopping. You'll get to the stage when carrying it up the hill is too much.'

I cut him off stiffly, 'I can still walk and still cart my own shopping,' too stiffly, 'but thanks.'

'Keep you safer and you wouldn't want to get into a scrap with that girl, would you,' he fishes.

We pause. His coffee is cool enough. He swallows it in one, starts to turn away from the window, away from the glare, then spots a shiny SUV pulling out from the side road, across the bridge.

'The Christians from the Manor. *Blessed by God*, it says on their gate,' I tell him.

'Really?'

'Yep. Seem like nice folk though, in that well-scrubbed, wholesome, kind of way. The kids do at least, the oldest gives me a wave when they pass. When her mother's not looking.'

The dawdling girl watches as the car passes without slowing, without so much as a nod or a finger wave. Once it's out of sight she slows her already slow dawdle to a loiter and veers toward the short steep driveway, that wanders through a garden full of cabbages draping the slope before a shady cottage.

'She often pops in there. Never stops for long.'

He loses interest once the girl disappears and glances back over his shoulder. 'Park's filling up,' he notes.

'Aye, couple of tents, couple of vans. Another week or two and she'll be chocka with the unwashed and undesirable.'

'You mean like you.'

'Aye,' I nod my appreciation, 'no good bludgers most of the year. I expect they'll be a few chancers among them selling this, that and the other.'

He watches as a tired camper with a high roof pulls in. It lumbers close to the road. The rear doors swing open, a black dog bounds out, two people set up a canopy to shade a few bits of furniture.

'Already here old man.'

He only visits once a month. Not often enough for what happens along the Lane to be normal. But he brings me what I can't get in the shops and makes an effort. He also seems to like my paintings, even if he doesn't understand them. But I can see that he hasn't let my shiner go and will bring it up again before he leaves.

'What have you got today?' I ask with an eager spark.

He reaches for his backpack, 'there's half an ounce there.'

'Nice,' I open the ziplock bag, take in the musty aroma. It's old, but still has a bit of a sticky funk. I put a good pinch in the bowl and shove the rest into my dressing gown pocket.

'End of the season, but should keep you going for a bit. Till yours is ready'

'I can tell. Good enough, thanks.' I load the bong that stands next to the easy chair, as tall as and half as wide as the easy chair. A car starts up down below. The motor sounds rough. An old European station wagon pulls away from a pretty little cottage. My neighbour, except for the fact I'm up the top of the hill, at the top of a long steep rutted driveway that only he dares to drive up. Otherwise we might be proper neighbours. But then she seems to be always busy tidying the house and gardening. Between the kid, house and garden, I don't think she ever stops.

The station wagon fumes and coughs down the road. I light the bong and fume and cough into the morning. I slide it over to him. Like an emphysemic's oxygen bottle it rumbles on casters, across the bare wooden floor. He takes a small toke to be sociable. He's not supposed to smoke. Not because of his health. Well sort of. The woman he lives with doesn't approve and would likely impact on his health, emotionally if not physically, if she caught him.

I tug the bong back, take another toke and roll it back to him. He says no then takes a toke, then another. He coughs again. I put the kettle back on, rinse the pot, fill it up, wait, plunge, pour and splash cold milk in his. We sit by the window in the fug. Silent. We both break the silence at the same time.

'When did...'

'How's your... you first,' I tell him and pack another bong.

'When did you get that?' He motions at my eye. 'Not the Christians I hope.'

I feel around my right eye. 'A couple of weeks back. And I won't be helping anyone again in a hurry. Now how are the kids, still doing as their mum tells them?'

'Yep.' He replies with a punctuating pop.

'You too?' I look straight at him. He smiles one of those smiles that says don't start. So I don't but skate the bong back toward him. He smokes. I smoke. We watch. We don't speak.

'Going to show me your latest work?'

Aye, of course,' we rise, 'that's what you come for really, isn't it.'

'Of course,' he mimics my expression. 'Nothing to do with you, old man.'

We make our way to the studio. Well, it's really the other end of the lounge room and what used to be two bedrooms.

'I see you've started on the next bedroom,' he says, sliding through the gap in a skeletal stud wall.

I like open plan. Lets the light penetrate more space. Besides, I need to paint on something. 'Aye, I've another two bedrooms to go.' I shift a couple of paintings so he can see them better. All the same size: half a wall panel. I perch them uniformly against the stud frame. His gaze is snagged by my most gruesome. No people, just bits. Bits of people.

'That's a bit grim,' he says, standing back, as if knocked slightly of balance, but continuing to look.

'Aye, 4 by 2,' he looks at me puzzled, 'four limbs, two heads.'

'Looks like a bomb's gone off.'

'It does.'

'Finished any of them yet?'

'Still working on all of them. You know how I am with titles, can't settle and titles are the last thing. Numbers are easy. They mean nothing and everything.'

'I like this one,' he says moving along the wall.'

'Thought you might, 75. It's yours when it's done. But I have to get the beard right.'

'Thanks,' he says, a little embarrassed, 'but I'm not sure it will fit in the flat. Motor bikes are a bit man cave.'

'You mean, you know she won't like it.'

He ignores my jibe and concentrates on the next in line, an average picture of ordinary folk, salt of the earth, some might say, whatever that means.

'Just don't get this one. It's just so ordinary.'

'Ordinary folk at number 84.'

He returns to the gruesome painting, then to the scratched outline of a middle-aged woman with a bouffant hair do that I'm also struggling with. He passes over an overly tall skinny fellow, then on to a short monstrous creature with outsized limbs, before returning to the ordinary folk. 'You seem to have miscounted,' he says smugly.

'No just tired of counting. I got to thinking there are probably numbers that haven't been thought of yet, like there are places that haven't been built yet, lives not lived yet. I'm number 66, next door is 58, so where are the numbers between?'

He scratches his chin, where a goatee might be if he was in control of his own image. At lunch we eat a sandwich, ham, cheese, and tomato and talk about footy. We support the same crap team, that got more than a black eye on the weekend, so no argument there. As I see him to the door he probes again. 'It's not important,' I tell him, and we hug. 'Say hi to that daughter of mine,' I mutter with a conciliatory tone.

'I will.' He says with welcome warmth.

'Don't know what you see in her but I'm glad you do.'

He smiles, 'she works hard and is good at what she does.'

'Only because she never wants to dig her own vegies again.'

'She's a good mother too,' he digs back.

I start to dig back when the air fills with a distant whirring noise and a helicopter comes into view from the north. We both follow its path as it chops south.

'Lost hiker, or car crash, I hope.'

'You hope,' he questions stiffly with a tone that questions my hope.

'Could be worse, it's been really dry lately.'

He softens, and calls back at me, as he spins his little car around 'I'll work it out you know.'

We yell our goodbyes and float smiles of affection and resignation in our waves. He rolls slowly down the hill and I settle down to paint what I can't see.

92 Cherrystone Lane

— *now*

Blind Eric

Blind Eric is conducting an experiment. He has no idea how long it will last, when it will end or what the result will be. He is, reasonably, confident he will live to see the end of it.

Eric travels the tracks, spurs and cuttings of the high-country park, over which the sun slips away from the valley. A short stocky man, with big hands and a deep roaring laugh, Eric cuts the figure of a kindly if not cuddly man. The kind one would be happy to come across on a mountain track. He knows his way around the park like the back of his hand, which is as hairy as the park is wooded and could probably find his way around it if he really was blind.

As a teenager he was told, on account of his big hands and fat fingers, that he was more suited to manual work than intellectual endeavours. His liking for animals slid him further down the career opportunity ladder and there weren't many conditions, in those days, with often tossed around acronyms, to explain just not being bookish.

Eric got over it quickly and has worked all his life at the same job. He knows no other and could most likely do no other. Indeed, he has never had any desire to do any other job. Now he has no desire to do the job he has done for the last 40 years.

For the first 30 years Eric enjoyed his job. He learned the job on the job and through books with pictures, mostly about animals and plants. He is proud of the knowledge and experience he's gained. He can tell you about every animal, bird, tree, moss, or lichen, that has strayed across his path, and many literally have. He knows when they will breed or blossom, when they will retreat, what eats what, where things live and what lives with what. He also knows when and where the odd itinerant camper will pitch up and has a gentle way of moving them on.

He is, mostly, happy about the people he's worked with and those he's met along the way. Eric got along with nearly all his workmates that kept him company as they bashed along the rutted roads, clearing tracks of tumbled rocks, fallen trees, or snapped limbs, counting birds, animals and noting blooms.

There was one young fellow that whinged a lot about the cold, the bumps in the road and why he couldn't drive, that seemed to have no interest in the park, the animals, the trees, or the fresh air. Eric tried to engage him and get him interested, but after six months of whinging, wanting to stop for a smoke every half hour and a pee every hour, Eric simply forgot to wait for him one day when he went into the bush for number twos.

Since then, things have changed a lot. The park is the same, full of the same sprouts, blooms, animals, birds, and campers, but it's lonesome work now. All Eric knows has no one to go to, there is no one to listen, no one to argue and discuss with, no one to laugh with. Eric sends in his reports and that's that. He thinks he might as well send in his favourite song of the week. Then he remembers a very serious fellow that rode around with him for a couple of years, that thought some of the bands he listened to and some of the titles of their songs sounded like new species of honey eaters, or pandani palms and spent weeks scanning for them. So he gave that idea the flick. An idea was seeded though, and Eric began to wonder what the point was. Was there a point. Would anyone notice if he stopped doing his job.

It's been three years now since Eric stopped doing his job and started doing nothing. Which is not entirely true. You see Eric made a garden, a wonderful garden at his home in the second darkest spot along Cherrystone Lane.

Eric's house is perched on a shelf, cut into the side of a steep hill of dense, almost, impenetrable bush, of looming stringy barks, spindly myrtle, and rotting tree ferns. Or put another way, in the prose of the local real estate agent, 'fragrant bush, alive with the marvels of nature'. Either way it's so bereft of sun that no one wants to buy it, and Eric has been trying to sell it since he started doing nothing at work.

He thought if his plan worked out, and no one noticed that he hasn't been doing his job, then instead of patrolling the park he'd sell up and patrol the park that is the big island to the north in his van that sits mostly idle in the garage. There are though only two hours during the day when the sun fills part of the house, less in winter, and most folk smelt a rat, a cold, dark, damp rat, when they were told viewings are strictly between 3.30 and 5 PM despite the fragrant bush alive with the marvels of nature.

So Eric works on his garden and grows more leafy greens than is imaginable. All in a big cage, or behind fences, so that the cuddly creatures up the hill, nature's marvels, can't decimate it. Where he doesn't grow cabbages, collards, spinach and chard, mushrooms, of many colours and shapes emerge. He thinks if he has a nice garden folk will think it's a sunny spot. Not many are taken in.

When Eric isn't in the garden he drives the park, like he used to when he was working, checking the roads and tracks are clear, recording wildlife sightings, flora observations and moving on itinerant campers. He finds the roads are rarely blocked, or seem to clear themselves, he makes up flora and fauna observations, or cuts and pastes them from years gone by and stops for a cuppa or beer, depending on the time of day, sometimes lunch with campers. Eric enjoys a good chat, especially about the park, and has a way of getting visitors to appreciate the park in the same way he does.

Most of all Eric loves the wombats, that dig their burrows in the park. He knows where every burrow is and has gathered a huge collection of wombat scat that he keeps in shoe boxes at home, each cube wrapped in foil paper like little sweet lozenges. Many campers have grown to understand that if they too love wombats Eric is a mate. So they keep an eye out for the lumbering creatures and report them to Eric when he stops. Some even collect scat for him. In return Eric turns a blind eye to folk pitching up for a few days and when they move on, which is by unspoken agreement in seven days, they make sure no evidence of their presence remains.

'I'll be seeing you in a week or two,' folk sing out to Eric, as he finishes his beer and climbs back into his government ute.

'And I'll not be seeing you, old mate,' he roars with a wide wave and broad grin.

On his way down from the park, on what Eric planned would be his last day, he is delayed with many goodbyes. He feels a responsibility toward the folk that have sort of made the park their home. Through summer to autumn there are quite a few. Usually older folk, many single women, finding their way, after divorce they never saw coming, or traumatised old men, rebuilding their core, after redundancy they never saw coming, the occasional lost young soul finding a way and, most rare, young families seeking a better path, or simply any path. Most have come to know Eric well, as the kindly old man that enjoys their company as much as his favoured wombats and, like them, knows when to move along.

Many were saddened, some mourn-full, some panicked. If they got a new ranger, how would he or she take to their unknown and unexpected wildlife.

It was two elderly women that came up with the answer. While Eric travelled, they offered to take the expected photographs, gather other data and send it to him. Then he could simply forward it for processing, as he had been doing.

This happy arrangement makes Eric late coming down the mountain. Which means he misses the last roast chook at the truck stop and since a sliver of the park has been opened up for logging, there's been a run on pies and battered morsels. Eric is a bit peeved about the sliver, pies, and morsels. He knows that once logged it is usually sold off for little blocks of fake farms, which means less space for all the creatures of the park and unexpected space in his groaning pot belly.

Again, Eric turns a blind eye and begins to think about what's in his freezer. All the way home he thinks about the cardboard pizza, with a measly scattering of reconstituted things, like he had the last time the takeaway shop was empty or closed. He isn't happy. For Eric, takeaway food, at least, means someone has cooked and packed it for him. He can't get that from frozen pizza.

Resigned to his soulless supper, as he turns into the Lane, he glides around the first bend, just before the first bridge, then sighs and slabbers in one movement at the sight of a green high roofed food truck throwing open its doors on a little patch of parkland. He breaks, pulls on to the verge, reads the hand scrawled sign and orders three sticks of meat and a burger.

'You know you're a life saver, thought I was stuck with cardboard pizza,' he explains to the pasty looking cook tending a heavy hot plate over a smoky fire.

200 Cherrystone Lane
— not long ago

Subsidence

Two hundred Cherrystone Lane, the old house beneath the pines, is sinking. It's the last house, before a rattly bridge, where the lane splits and climbs stiffly up the hill to where the land has been scrubbed of trees and scarred by fire. There a few old timber getters huts stand defiant along with desperate caravans, that once kindled dreams but now moulder in abandonment.

Those that climb its rutted track, are mostly hooking wood from stream sides or steep slopes, protected on paper or beyond the reach of mechanical harvesters, or tipping their detritus for the bushy slopes to swallow.

At 200 Cherrystone Lane the rivulet is absent. Here the rivulet is ignored. An inconvenience noted at the bridge where the garbage has to be trundled to and the removalists have to decant their ill-fitting jumble, the possessions of the oldest woman of the house. Plopped into the back of a rusted ute, with less care, less felted fending cloth, they are shuttled: boxes, chairs, a bed, a TV, and trousseau, in five journeys, along a thin dirt track to the warmest room in the dank house.

Elizabeth too is shuttled and installed in the same room. At eighty, she does not walk far and gave up walking further than the kitchen and bathroom from her chair or bed, at sixty-eight. She is always Elizabeth too, not Liz, or Lizzy, 'I don't have scales,' she used to spit, when diminished. Neither is she Beth or Betty.

At sixty-eight she had both knees and one hip replaced. The last time she spoke was a year later to curse all three. 'I'm not one for foreign, modern or new fandangled ways,' she used to often say. Which always got a head shake from her granddaughter and a giggle from her great granddaughter. Yet it was a foreign doctor, and new technology that raised her from the dead, following the haemorrhagic stroke that left her shuffling and speechless.

Elizabeth's room is the only renovated room in the house. It is on the high side, that is it is sinking more slowly, but also in the darkest corner. The paint and plasterboard are new, as is the lush emerald carpet, fitted over ancient, scalloped floorboards. The remainder of the old house is lined with wide split celery top pine slabs and the same floorboards, that rise and fall like a brooding sea, sucking in a rank draft where there are no rugs and echo to the scurry of scuttling rats that travel well established canals beneath.

Elizabeth brought her own curtains and insisted that was the first box opened. She directed their hanging, with blunt fists distorted by swollen knuckles, from her tapestried armchair, pointing silently in agitated mime. She was always agitated, like there was a temper of explosive force trapped inside.

She had no wish to see the outside, the unkempt garden, or pond that bred squadrons of mosquitoes among dense plumes of bulrushes, that filled most of its surface and drew an afternoon breeze fanning white fluff at her window. The pond is the confluence of springs that thread-like veins, unhealthy varicose veins, through the property, beneath and around the house, before flowing under the Lane to the rivulet, where the tall pines, a thicket of willow and tangle blackberry drink thirstily.

Elizabeth is thin. She's been thin all her life. Her shape has not changed just sagged. Only her knuckles grew fat. The middle joint of her fingers so swollen her rings are fixed and roll loosely as washers on bent bolts, above them. Her hair, also thin, straight, and always long past her bony shoulders, is kept tied back, pinned in a silver bun, when she is good, and just tied back at other times.

Liz is the next oldest and it is her house. Despite how the others treat it, calling it their house, my house, instead of Mum's, or Gran's.

Liz had married well, as they used to say about marrying money. Her husband lived well, too well, and succumbed to the lifestyle excesses that tested most members of heavy metal bands.

After her rock star, Liz had a succession of partners, but none could match the fame that she bathed modestly in. Only Ron, a sometime artist, lathe driver and turner of round things, came close. Her fascination for spinning chunks of wood seduced her and produced a second child, a boy child. But the praise of all things wood and round led Ron and Ron junior to an obscure cult in which the epicentres of wooden bowls were meditated upon and thought to hold deep secrets. So Ron and son retreated to his parent's farm on the north coast of NSW.

This was Liz's last roll of the dice that had tumbled sometimes well and sometimes not. The comfortable harbour side apartment on the edge of a mainland city, was sacrificed for a twee dilapidated cottage of rotten weatherboard in the suddenly trendy Huon Valley. An out of the way pocket at the end of the world where she could care for her mum, placate her flaky daughter and try to manage her granddaughter, that took too much after her grandfather.

After years of socialiting, on royalties and a moderately successful lingerie shop, Liz was taken by the sea or tree change, or just the need for change, that afflicts people of a certain age. Her enthusiasm for relative isolation, peace and quiet and nature, was sustained for one and half rooms, a garden clearance and terrace design. It flagged at the bathroom when the septic tank gurgled brown sludge back at her and flooded the newly cleared garden. The pond, fortunately, or unfortunately, acted as a supplementary overflow and settlement reservoir.

Fixing the sewage outfall swallowed the last of her savings. In turn, saving the four women from the embarrassment of slopping through their own muck and being taken to court for polluting the rivulet. Liz made the best of it. Her pension would pay the bills and her daughter and granddaughter would just have to help out.

Beth is a keen worker as long as she wants to do it. Which is anything for five minutes. If a task requires extended focus Beth's smile falls to a frown that soon emits a whine, a whine that dribbles from nostrils that seem to have been smacked onto the face that gives them rise, in little piggy fashion. Elizabeth has little time for her granddaughter. A flaky fool, she thinks of her, a difficult person she used to speak of her, and when in Liz's company she agrees of her father's making.

Beth is a stumpy and often grumpy woman. Talent is her challenge. She believes she has it, she just needs time to find it. At forty-two, she is not ready to give up and believes she is entitled to keep looking. How could she live her life without realising what she must have inherited from her father. And there are still many creative expressions she's not tried.

Music was naturally her first exploration. She took up the flute at ten before finding her lips didn't hang that way, so picked up a harmonica before noting how ugly she looked trying to summon enough in and out breath. The guitar was too cliched and drums, although in the blood, hard work and took up too much space. Modelling she thought next, then a well-worn path to acting and persuaded her mother to invest thousands on drama classes.

Moon chanting was her most enduring interest. Although her father was little more than a drummer in a rock 'n roll band, she just needed to sing and banging a goat skin drum while wailing and dancing half naked around a circle of believers, keen for their spirits to be cleansed, seemed to somehow draw many of her talents together, while also channelling the spirit of her father. Full moons often drew a paying crowd and her audience, or community as she liked to call it, grew. Then she started to paw each member and more and more the close community became too close for many and eventually closed.

Since moving to the Lane, with her mum, gran and daughter, Beth has become newly interested in ceramics, digging clay from the banks of the rivulet, making moulds of her own body parts and trying to convince the rest of the household to let her mould theirs. Beth is nothing if not derivative. Elizabeth refused with furrowed brow and a clunk of her clawed hand. Liz ummed and arred. She always wanted to encourage her daughter in her artistic quests and Betty simply asked, 'how much?'

At fourteen, 'how much?' became Betty's mantra. It would see her well and led to an outlook on life that left her with few friends and less love. 'How much?' she asked one of her mother's clients, before sleeping with him for drugs. Her mother tried to keep her close, taken in by eyes that drooped with sympathy, seemed constant with tears and in their spilling wrote and undeniable plea.

Beth loved her. How could she not love the only child of her womb, the result of a promise of a part in a TV soap. Liz loved her but didn't like her. Elizabeth, in her silence, wished her dead and made that quite clear with a deathly scowl and tight rolled fists when she came near.

At ten Betty was close to her great grandmother. She brushed her straight silver locks each night, before lacing them in plaits around her crown. She idolised her style, her elegance, her glamour. Most of all she loved her frocks.

Elizabeth loved to see Betty in her dresses, insisting on setting them off with the right necklace, earrings, and brooches. Elizabeth had also married well, but not above her station, for Elizabeth was born to class, if modest wealth.

At fourteen Betty wandered into her mother's circle, retreating, when things weren't going well, to her great grandmother. A year later she ran away. Two years later she returned and two years later still most of Elizabeth's jewels were gone. Gradually Elizabeth's savings dwindled to nothing. Liz had to pay for her medical costs. It was the stroke and Liz's guardianship of her mother's affairs that saved Elizabeth from the streets and Betty from jail.

Still Betty remains within the safety and tolerance of blood, working hard to stay close to Gran. Liz, while the most difficult to charm, is the most forgiving and caring. Mum is decaying from an undiscussed cancer, a metastatic mass, that she believes is the seat of her talent, and Great Gran could be expected to pass on soon, and pass on whatever remained of her wealth, some of which might just trickle down.

Betty knows she's siphoned off most but there is always the chance that there might be a hidden property, or insurance policy and there are those rings, guarded by those arthritic knuckles. In the meantime, the small community of Cherrystone Lane might yield some friends for the making. Then there is the wider community, the little town over the hill, the one upriver and the one across the river, that might yield some dumb and decaying folk for the taking.

Betty living with her mother is, like the others living under the one roof, dependent on Liz, who is responsible for keeping her mum warm, her daughter happy and her granddaughter out of jail and attending therapy.

Elizabeth spends her days in front of the TV, furiously chopping channels between the three that can be received beneath the shadow of giant pine trees. For the time being Beth is moulding parts of her body with stinky clay and baking them in a wood fire out the back. Some survive the firing process but most crack and crumble on handling, or a day or two later. Still Beth persists. Both Elizabeth and Liz are most impressed as Beth continues into the third week. With the aid of careful balance and stick props a brittle half torso of the maker is taking shape, just as the rounded shape of the maker is falling away.

Betty didn't care about her mum's art or her mum but did tell her she was looking good as the weight loss became noticeable. Betty was out two days a week, set out along the road by Liz. Less than an old-fashioned mile to the bus stop Liz arranged for checkins at the therapy centre and the police station her granddaughter had to report to. Liz thought the walk would do Betty good. Give her time to reflect and get her life together. 'She really is a good girl,' Liz said to herself as she forced the front door closed.

The Lane tracks the rivulet along to the highway where the bus shelter, a little three-sided tin shed, facing the road and also facing the weather is set. Despite living at 200 Cherrystone Lane, there are only a few other houses along the road: a newly renovated cottage across the rivulet, a cute place above the road with a lovely garden of cabbages, a steep muddy track, an orchard, and a vacant block, with a falling down barn, facing away from the weather, and a bit of a park. Betty gave them names, Waterfront Cottage, Cabbage Patch House, Wedgewood Cottage, after the crockery collection her Great Gran once had, Broken Barn and so on. At the orchard house she scrumped a couple of fat yellow pears from trees that overhung the road. She took a massive bite and quickly spat it out. The cottage on the rivulet worried her a bit, with the deep mechanical thumps that interfered with the babbling water, but she took comfort in the rivulet as a barrier. The garden with all its cages and netting and big leaves confused her, but the mushrooms made her curious. She came to notice that on sunny days the car, a government vehicle, was gone. She climbed the drive and kicked around the garden. She knew of some mushrooms but not enough of them. She'd need to find out more.

On the sixth day of passing, and the car being gone, Betty wanders into the house. Like most places along the Lane, it isn't locked. The kitchen is tidy, with few signs of use, other than coffee, toast, and a tower of neatly stacked takeaway containers.

In the lounge a single easy chair, opposite a TV. The room next door, darker than the rest of the house, offers more intrigue. A laptop computer sits atop a desk with two deep draws. She tucks the laptop under her arm and opens the top drawer. The usual detritus greets her, pens, scraps of paper, broken pencils. She pulls the bottom draw open, expecting nothing more, lifts out a shoebox, opens it and is dazzled by the little silver wrapped cubes.

'Bingo,' she smiles, peeling back the silver paper from one lozenge, sniffs it, nibbles it, 'smells like shit, tastes like shit, but looks like hash.' She closes the door and walks home, shoebox under her arm.

As the days stretch out the light eeks meekly into the house. The household takes on a lightness all around. Beth has given up on clay, returning to her moon chanting practice and other healing therapies. Betty is still attending therapy, albeit with increasing disgruntlement. Liz is keeping it all together and Elizabeth staying mostly in her room, rises regularly at mid-day to watch TV. Then Liz receives news that Ron has turned his last bowl and turned up his toes. While they have been estranged for many years his funeral does offer the opportunity to reconnect with Ron junior. She makes arrangements to travel and instructs Beth in the running of the house. Beth being Beth allows her ego to accept the responsibility, while at the same time thinking it will be a breeze as there isn't much to do and that she can manage her expanding business at the same time.

So the chanting, reiki, chakra straightening, drumming circle and mindfulness coaching commences on the night Liz left and continued through the weekend. On Monday morning Betty jams her clothes into a rucksack and marches along the Lane for the last time, pack on her back, shoebox under arm. Her mother didn't see the going of her, just the usual forcing of the heavy door into the less than door shaped hole indicating her daughter's departure.

The slam disturbs her momentarily. Soon she drifts back to sleep and having given deeply of her inner self, for the goodness of others over the weekend she sleeps through the day and long into the evening. She wakes only for the toilet and long enough to make a cup of herbal tea. She listens fleetingly at Elizabeth's door as she passes. The TV is still on. She then goes back to sleep until early the next morning, when Liz kicks open the front door, that always sticks after being slammed shut. Mother and daughter greet each other in the hallway and listen to the TV, still blathering away in Elizabeth's room.

Two smiling faces glare luridly from the screen as the two women enter. Elizabeth is slumped awkwardly in her chair, her head lolling, tongue, that last muscle to sag, sagging, eyes staring and fingers as if gnawed off by the rats.

58 Cherrystone Lane

— soon

Wedgwood Cottage

Jason and Kylie bought Wedgwood Cottage three years ago, during a mass exodus from the close confines and sickness of the city, rush to leafy greenness, space, fresh air, and the ability to work from home. Two years later Jason was summoned back to the office, stifling heat, air conditioning and a long commute. Neither Jason nor Kylie wanted to return. He enjoyed his spacious office in the second bedroom, did more work in a day than he ever did corralled behind three office partitions and got to spend more time with Kylie.

She spent those two years filling the house with beautiful things, mostly gathered from online reproduction factories and home decor outlets. Deliveries were frequent at the smart little cottage. Soon the space was nicely cluttered, including the third bedroom, cutely furnished for a baby expected in six months.

The call to return to the office was unexpected and unwelcome. It was thought by many at the onset that working from home would be the new norm. But the reflex of business, to control and observe, to improve productivity, quickly returned to the boardrooms. Jason and Kylie discussed the idea of quitting and finding work that would allow them to stay but nothing matched his salary, or status, and he always said he had the perfect job that would see them secure for the rest of their lives. So, with great reluctance, they moved back to the city, to the office, to her parents' place, while her parents continued to live in the shack that was really a well-appointed beach house.

They promised each other that they would return to Wedgwood Cottage for holidays and when he was senior enough to work from home and they could afford it permanently.

Lilly and Lulu moved into Wedgwood Cottage in July, just as the first light dusting of snow settled on the manicured lawn. The neat weatherboard house always looked like there was a piping of snow, like icing on the gutter, roof flashing, timber finials and trim and the light fall of snow extended this effect against the powder blue weatherboards.

Lilly loves the house every bit as much as Kylie, while Lulu is at home wherever her mother is. The old station wagon Lilly parked in the driveway carries everything they own. From the outside it's a smart European car: one of those you could comfortably stretch out in. On the inside it has that clean but lived in look.

The first thing Lilly did was clean the kitchen, then the bathroom. Not just wiping the surfaces but scrubbing, getting into the grout between the tiles with a toothbrush. Lilly is meticulous in her housekeeping, maintaining the place in spotless condition. Such is her obsession that she and Lulu sleep in the little granny flat out the back so as not to disturb the museum like interior of the cottage.

Lilly's obsession extends to the garden, where autumn leaves barely settle, shrubs are neatly pruned, roses deadheaded before death and the corkscrew parcels of wallaby poo are swept daily from the lawn that the wallabies, in their nighttime passing, nibble down to a cricket pitch neatness.

Lulu started school. Lilly drives her in the morning and collects her every afternoon. At five years old, even with, or perhaps because of, her smoky complexion and loose curls she makes friends easily but knows never ever to invite friends home. For mother and daughter school is school, home is home, and they don't mix any more than the neighbours along the Lane are welcome into their immaculate home.

Every second Friday, after dropping Lulu off, Lilly shops. First at charity shops where she picks up day old bread, sometimes cake, sometimes homemade jam, sometimes eggs, and occasionally something nice for Lulu, a pretty top, a toy, or a book. Then to the supermarket where rice and pasta are the first stop. Then whatever meat and veg is on special. Sometimes she is lucky and finds a nearly out of date chicken that she knows will be a bit smelly when liberated from its sweaty plastic skin and in need of a good wash in some vinegar. Mostly she gets mince, or a bag of dog bones to make mutton stew, a big bag of carrots, potatoes and tinned tomatoes and corn.

There is never much money left after shopping and putting the rest aside to pay the electricity bill, and winter chews a lot of that, which also makes living mostly in the granny flat very sensible. Most other days she cleans house. Even if the house is spotless there is always dust. Like the leaves from the silver birches that hide the house from the road and are supposed to catch the dust, it is never allowed to settle.

In the school holidays they explore the bush that goes up the hill behind the house. There are vague tracks, overgrown paths that look as if they've not been used for ten years or so, because skinny wattles are sticking up in the middle. When they come to little clearings where trees have fallen and grass now grows, they pause, eat a bit of cake, have a drink of water and Lulu plays a game of setting out where they would build a little house, away from everyone. Away from the world.

'And we can have a garden here,' she calls, stretching out her arms, 'and a little house here for a puppy.'

Then they walk on, always aiming for the top of the hill but never reaching it, before mother and daughter are worn out or the path gets too steep, or the bush too thick.

'Next time,' Lilly consoles Lulu, 'next time we will go all the way to the top. Next time we will find the perfect place for a puppy.'

I heard them one time. They'd strayed on to the back of my place. There's a nice hollow there where the bush gives way to a little saucer shaped clearing. She used to play there with friends before she got all serious. It was nice to hear a child's voice in the bush again chirruping like birdsong skittling through the trees.

On the way down the hill, just as the bush gives way to a cleared slope, before the granny flat, they hear a sharp tap on the door at the side of the house.

'Hello, it's Eric from next door.' The man speaks loudly through the lead light window, 'I just wondered if you'd seen anyone snooping around my place?'

'Shoosh,' Lilly beckons her daughter, and they duck back into the bush, 'it's the short little man that drives the government vehicle. Quiet, till he's gone,' she whispers.

They watch the neighbour toddle down the drive on his stumpy little legs. When he's at the gate Lulu turns to her mother. 'He looks like a fat little puppy dog.' Together they stifle a laugh before continuing down the hill.

'Are we in trouble again mum?' Lulu asks.

'No darling, he's just a neighbour.'

That evening after dinner, which is always eaten in the kitchen, they sit in the lounge and watch the big television. They do this most evenings but on Saturday they watch an extra hour and always the commercial channels. Lilly thinks the others are too posh and too serious. Lulu loves the TV and sits cross legged on the thick carpet inching closer and closer, as if she's never seen anything in such detail before. Until Lilly tuts, which means Lulu shuffles back, half as far as she's shuffled forward.

Every Sunday morning Lilly does the laundry, and every Sunday afternoon is bath time. Lulu's allowed to play in the bath for half an hour but not splash. If there's water or suds on the bathroom floor she is told off and five minutes taken off the next Sunday's bath time.

'We need to keep the place as nice as it was when we found it,' Lilly always says, following a few harsh words.

'Yes mummy. I'm sorry.'

During bath time, the following Sunday, Lilly hears the gate open and a car pull into the driveway.

Lulu calls out, 'Is it the neighbour again Mummy?'

Lilly lifts Lulu out of the bath, 'stay here and dry yourself.'

As she approaches the front door, drying her hands, she hears a key slide into the lock. 'Lulu stay where you are and lock the door.' The bolt slides across the bathroom door as the front door opens.

'Who the hell are you,' asks a blond man in the doorway. 'Kylie stay in the car and take care of Rosie.'

Lilly stands silently while the man flies into a mostly incoherent tirade. 'I want you out this minute. This is our house, how dare you....' Such is the anger rising in his veins that he breaks off and turning back to his wife and child starts again, 'Kylie call the police we've been....' Only an unseen interruption stems his anger.

'Mum, can I come out now?'

Not sure of the command Kylie leaves the car but not the toddler and scurries up the path in her heels, child on hip, 'Did you say call the police... and who the fuck is this in our house?' She pulls her child close to her and whispers an apology for her language. The child makes a reach for a small plastic bike, that sits neglected under the veranda. Kylie steps forward to threaten Lilly. Lulu comes up the hallway wrapped partly in a towel. 'Mummy-mummy I'm dry. Can I watch television.'

Kylie abbreviates her charge but not her wagging finger. 'What the...' she modifies her language, passes Rosie to Jason, and continues. Rosie makes another reach for the plastic tricycle.

'Go and put some clothes on Lulu. They're in the laundry. Then come right back.'

'Can I play then mum?' Lilly ignores the request.

Rosie continues her reach for the tricycle, Jason takes her over to it, sits her on it. She walks herself along the veranda. Her new wheels make a hollow rumble over the boards, then back, then she veers toward the doorway.

'Not in the house,' advises Lilly.

The child reverses down the veranda and onto the driveway. Kylie seethes but does not disagree. Jason is on the phone, terrible music going around and around interrupted by a brief message that finishes with 'as soon as possible.'

Kylie summons her daughter back, 'Rosie, get off of that. It's not yours.'

'It's okay,' Lilly speaks directly to the other mother for the first time, 'she doesn't use it much anymore.'

Kylie loses it. Jason restrains her. 'Get out of my house, you, you, you...,' the word is there but either won't, or can't make its way out with children around. She turns to Jason instead. He is still on hold, 'I feel, I feel,' again Kylie's anger retards her words, 'invaded. I feel violated. How dare you and that child.... Get whatever you have and get out of my house.' She takes a steadying breath. 'Where do you live?'

Lilly gestures to the station wagon, that is parked in and begins a defence, 'we had nowhere to go and it was empty and the laundry door was open and Lulu was cold.

'Oh, I see. Typical of you people. Poor child.' Kylie is managing to contain her anger, but it is building up beneath her infuriated complexion. 'Jason put that down, they probably won't come anyway. Go with her, get her things, and make sure she takes only her things. There couldn't be much. Then see her to her car. I'll move ours out of the way.' She turns, storms to the car on her click-clack heels, starts it, yells at Lilly out of the window. 'You're fucking lucky, you piece of...' releases the hand-break, slides the SUV into reverse, hits the accelerator and listens to the rest of her life, as the stretching snap and buckle of the plastic bike yields beneath the force of the car's bumper.

Her breath freezes. Her rage drains to hollow white. She slumps forward.

A tubby man waddles up the drive. 'Hello there, I'm from next door. I called in the other day.'

Lilly steps from the shadow of a line of trees that mark the driveway, a small blond child in her arms. Kylie runs to her. The child reaches for Kylie. Lilly passes the child. Kylie hugs the child, like she's just found her after a long search.

'I just wondered if you'd seen anyone snooping around my place,' the man continues, looking directly at Lilly, 'and if you could keep a look out. I'm going away for a long time, travelling, and the place will be empty. Anyway, sorry to interrupt. I didn't know you had family visiting. I'll leave you to get on.

100 Cherrystone Lane
– yesterday

Black Charlie's Opening

Black Charlie's guts growl, like the possum that danced on the roof last night. He doesn't gripe. He knows there's greater hunger. He's seen much of it in the corners of the world he stumbled into, not so many years ago.

Big Charlie passes him a tin mug of coffee, as dark and oily as the lubrication that keeps the old Land Rover rumbling on the equally dark and oily road. 'Next turning, pull in. Breakfast soon,' she orders.

Black Charlie is so pale he is often mistaken for an albino. Big Charlie slapped the black part on him when she told him he looked so sexy in his tight black jeans and matching body-hugging shirt that just held across his weedy chest. That was twenty years ago. Since that day he only wears black. In reply, he told her he loved her accent, born in the high peaks of Europe. He also loved her ample breasts, soon had fun with her unmissable butt and found her blue lippy and eye shadow irresistible. But he wanted to come across as a modern and sensitive man.

Since then, they've been in blissful transit. Not around Venus, or any other distant planet, but around the country and more recently the backroads of Tasmania. During this time Black Charlie has let his Mohawk grow out and the vibrant rainbow colours grizzle to grey. Big Charlie now keeps her blue lippy and eye shadow for special occasions, but maintains her natural jet-black bird's nest.

Black Charlie pulls over where the road widens, just after a junction, just before a wide white gated driveway that is the entrance to a paddock full of small horses and mini goats. The high roof of the camper catches a cross wind and sways. As Charlie climbs between the seats, into the back, it creaks on its springs and sways some more.

They don't speak. These are precious moments, before the little bundle of rags in the corner stirs and extends a groping mitt in silent demand for porridge. They consult the map between mouthfuls, planting fingers on forests and parks, neglected graveyards, lonely beaches and where they estimate camps they've been told about might be.

Black Charlie is measuring distance with two walking fingers. Big Charlie scoffs her porridge, sculls her tea, inverts her cup into her bowl, studies it, then points to the spot on the map that Black Charlie's finger has just stepped from. 'There,' she says emphatically.

Black Charlie doesn't argue, not because he always does as he's told but because it's less far than his fingers were stepping, and both he and Big Charlie are folk of few words. In the evenings, when folk speak most, she sews and he carves, or she cooks and carves while he breaks and trims and sews pelts together. Or they read, sometimes to each other, then clamber into the frontal lobe of the camper and make it rattle and sway again.

The bundle of rags, conceived in the bed on high and born onto the table below where they take breakfast, stirs slowly and is fed. Black Charlie finishes his coffee and climbs back into the driver's seat. They have another fifty clicks of good road to collect supplies. After that they are on the dirt and the road is clear and barren, on account of people driving more cautiously. They stop twice before the dirt to gather supplies and once along the forest track, to pick a few mushrooms and for Darko, growling in Black Charlie's ear, to take a pee.

They make camp at the end of a forest spur, where heavy boulders have been parked on a rise above a small stony creek, to keep the public out of public land. They are welcomed cautiously by others. Caution, they know, is a common state for those on the road and while, they often run into friends in different camps, there are ten times as many whose paths never cross.

Two elderly women, limited in their camp by the nature of their bus, are the first to say hello. Or rather it is the equally elderly Labrador, which sniffs Darko's butt.

'Been long here?' asks Big Charlie.

Millie, the heaviest, more forward and more open of the two women, tells her, 'Couple of weeks, nice and quiet,' then motions to the old Kombi in the other corner of the clearing. 'He's okay, quiet, keeps himself to himself. A bit simple if you ask me.' She introduces herself and Molly, her less forward travelling companion.

'Oh, and that's Puddle, he's old and been done.'

'Charlotte,' says Big Charlie, 'but friends call me Charlie, Big Charlie.' She gestures in the direction of the high-top camper, its vaguely military green blending in with the bush, where Black Charlie is setting a fire. 'That is too Charlie, Black Charlie and this'—she pats the Rottweiler at her knee—'is Darko. She's not so old but also'—she hesitates—'been done as you say.'

Black Charlie releases the chooks from the trailer. All girls. They'd had trouble when they kept a rooster. Other campers whining about disturbing the peace and quiet of nature. Charlotte usually had a piece of them, about nature not being quiet and often added something about being 'doomed because of you people'. To which Darko always concurred, as they retreated to their own wheels. Besides, Black Charlie has come to recognise that roosters tend to gather at a lot of out-of-the-way street corners, where travelling hens pass or stop. A lot like teenage boys. And that they could be relied on to make young chicks, if kept cramped in the trailer for a week or so. But you were always on the lookout, always on the move when you kept roosters, so it was best to turn them into a tasty broth, sooner rather than later.

With the hens out foraging, the fire smoking from under damp wood, Black Charlie draws his knives over a whetstone: a skinner, a boner, and a carver. He likes to think he has the sharpest knives for miles, but since they usually move every couple of days, or weeks at best, that's hard to prove.

Millie, at the behest of Molly, who spotted the chooks from beneath her shadows, calls out as Big Charlie is leaving. She begins with a friendly 'Big Char—' then as Big Charlie turns, transitions quickly to a formal Charlotte, asking if there might be a spare egg or two and says they're happy to pay or swap some bean sprouts. Charlotte scoffs at the offer, knowing that Charlie will feed the sprouts to the chooks, but that every dollar will buy fuel.

'There may be. We will see in the morning. Dollar each.'

Molly shakes her chins in hope and agreement. 'It's been a few weeks between eggs.'

Charlie has strung up one of the wallabies they collected on the road by the back legs and is heaving off the skin. Darko is already munching on the head. Puddle circles. Charlotte lends her weight to Charlie's struggle. Soon the carcass swings naked, lean, and purple.

As Charlie begins to butcher, opening up the paunch, Darko circles close. Puddle keeps a respectful distance. Charlie hooks out the giblets: heart and lungs, and tosses them to her, the liver to the older dog. They scoff their morsels in one. The carcass is soon boneless, and Charlotte is cranking the handle of an old cast-iron mincer while Charlie feeds it strips of lean purple meat. He stokes the fire and makes more smoke. Charlotte mixes the sticky flesh with oil and some yellow mushrooms.

The low rolling smoke raises the attention of the old man from the Kombi, the side door scuffing open. Charlotte glances over, with the usual caution of those on the road. Beneath wide bell-bottom jeans, that may have come from the original era of wide bottomed trousers, long dirty toenails dangle to earth. An old tartan blanket covers a pear-shaped torso, topped with a shrunken head, framed by an untamed beard and long, thin, greasy hair.

Charlotte doesn't like beards, especially long unkempt ones. She distrusts mostly bald men with beards and long thin greasy hair even more so. 'Child fiddlers,' she calls them and mutters as much, missing her alliteration.

Black Charlie spits on a hunk of heavy steel in the shape of a manhole grate. It sizzles loudly, he slaps on some patties. Slowly the old man limps closer, the kind of limp the result of a thorn in the foot, a thorn that would have to fester and burst out in its own time. The old man can't reach that far and is unlikely to find a volunteer. Darko growls at every untimely step.

'Is that wallaby there on the ... the ... the ...?' comes a hesitant inquiry, pointing, with a crooked finger to replace lost words.

'Yar,' snaps Charlotte.

'Not tasted wallaby in a long time,' slurs the grubby old man, rewrapping his blanket and peeling his hair from his face.

Charlie notices the tension. He understands Charlotte's stereotyping. 'I'll fetch you one over when they're done, old man.'

'That's very hosp ... hosp ...hosp—' The old man searches and stammers again but never gets there.

'Kind.' Charlotte completes his sentence slamming the mincer down on the block. At which point the old man retires to wait and Charlie has a word with Charlotte. A hundred times he's told her that in some dusty corners of world he's travelled folk would offer the old man food, if not shelter, and listen to his stories.

She accepts her ticking off but says she can't help it, as she has done a hundred times before, that she just has this feeling around some people, sometimes.

That evening, while Charlotte reads a book, about hermits in the outback, borrowed from one of those little free community book exchanges, Charlie cuts a cross into a sheep's skull, right between and just above where the eyes would have been. Through the gradual abrasion of bone, he makes a window in the shape of a crucifix, then sets about cutting away the bone at the back of the head. He inserts a small tea candle, lights it, and sits it on the bonnet of the camper they call home. The skull shines a weak light. Charlotte thinks it enough to ward off evil spirits, or filthy, straggle-haired men with bushy beards. It also keeps the possums off the roof that night.

In the morning six chooks deliver five eggs. Charlotte delivers two to Millie and Molly, returning with two dollars she deposits in a biscuit tin they keep under the passenger seat. A shallow tin, with a picture of a cute, homely cottage, surrounded by rolling fields of sheep and cattle, on the lid. She always pauses to take in the picture before prising the lid off. They know the tin holds seventy-six dollars when full. Enough to fill the tank with petrol. They're both half full.

Millie and Molly are so grateful that they perform a strange, coordinated, almost religious ceremony. First the toasting of two slices of homemade bread till they are dry and crumbly, buttering and vegemiting, then slicing into strips before, in perfect time together, beheading the eggs—since boiled for three minutes—and inserting said toasted, buttered and vegemited strips into the yolk and into gobs. The ceremony causes both women to close their eyes in blissful delight as they macerate the dark, glossy, eggy strips.

Charlotte looks on in wonderment at their deliberateness and pleasure, the simple pleasure two eggs have yielded.

'There's folk more poor than us,' whispers Charlie.

Shady is up early for Shady. Shady walks but never talks, not a single word in five years. When they are on the move Shady dozes, lulled to sleep by the mostly regular rumble of the engine and wheels turning over the road. When they aren't on the road Shady walks in the forest, around the camp, or along the beach in the morning, mostly with Darko for company. In the afternoon Shady does schoolwork. Well, he draws pictures, of what he's seen in the morning. Today he draws tall trees with a bent witch's hat mountain in the distance and a little creek in the foreground. All with thick black outlines. Charlie and Charlotte are of the opinion that if he can relate to his environment, the place where he lives, he is learning and will be alright. Even if his environment changes from day to day, week to week. For Charlie and Charlotte, the most important thing is to not let him be taken away.

On the second day camp is made more comfortable. Charlie strings up a canopy from the camper, propping it up with a couple of bush poles. Charlotte sweeps and spreads a few skin rugs on the dirt. Supplies last a week, before the dried rations begin to get the better of them.

The old man in the Kombi moves on two days in and Millie and Molly pack up the day after, but not before buying two more eggs and telling Charlotte the extensive story of how they came to be on the road. Which, in short, is Molly's sensitivity to electric light. But like the road, stories go on, especially when Milly is doing the telling and Molly is always a long time squatting in the bush.

'You see Molly grew up in the city but had to get out. She loved people and crowds. Just as she loves your candle in a skull.'

'Ghost light,' corrects Charlotte.

'But she got sick more and more, but the more she went into the bush the more the headaches stayed away. No one believed her. Some bought her curtains. But it was more than the light. It's the residue, the fallout into everything. Like the air is charged with light, long after the light has burned out. Like everything it touched. Everything it's shone upon is charged and burned. Molly calls it her damning. Others call it her drama-ing. Then her skin flaked, her hair was constant static and attracted to every artificial fibre. Her eyes itched and the itch smelled of piss ants. Now she only sees in pixels.'

Only Millie believed Molly. So she bundled her into the back of her camper and drove her, as fast as she could, as far as she could, from neon, far from halogen, far from fluorescence, far from optic poison, to the darkest skies in the country.

Eggs and dried beans are not getting Charlie off to a good start in the morning, and the coffee is getting thin too. Charlotte is drinking tea made from the local ground cover and Shady is drawing in the dirt and scratching trees. Only Darko is doing well.

They would have gone south to where the beaches are many and people few, where they could back into the still damp forest, listen to the waves crashing on the rocks across the road and forage along the coast. But the crayfish season is starting at the weekend and the fisher folk, in their salt-haggard utes, leaky caravans and tinny boats, with their beer and generators, will be swamping the place. And that is going to be too much facial hair and too much thin hair beneath too many dodgy beanies for Charlotte.

The high mountain park, on the other hand, will be quiet, and the water from the river, sweet. You have to be careful going in, the track is slow, narrow and steep, and there isn't much room once you get in, so not many folk go there.

Hunting and trapping is good too, if you get desperate. There isn't much veg in the park but lots of fresh water and mountain air, which makes it ideal for drying meat. Two weeks in the mountain breeze sets salted strips of wallaby to tough pliable straps that last forever. Charlie makes good hardtack and carves bones.

Charlotte finishes her book about methylated hermits up north and together they make up stories, based on Shady's drawings, about how they live and where they live, and Darko brings home some meat, until they set off again.

As they re-enter the freeway the utes and boats and battered caravans of the crayfish folk speed by on the other side of the freeway.

'End of the weekend,' chorus Charlie and Charlotte.

The beach would be okay now, but Charlie has other ideas. Continuing to where the crayfish folk came from, slowly, they meander along the narrowing road. Slowly, they gather the carnage left by those that hurried from the beach just as they'd hurried to it. Before the beach, way before, he takes a left and drives an hour in, along a rough track, through tea tree swamp that wakes Shady from his usual slumber and has Darko, even on four legs, working hard to stay balanced, until they come to a wide lagoon and busy camp of small fires, vans, and tents. Half-a-dozen boats, of dull grey shell, litter the shore; the smell of fish lifts with the smoke out of smouldering hearths of stone and mud. Sooted children chase each other with lighted sticks and fragile skeletons.

The loft of the Land Rover brushes branches of spindly gumtrees. Half-a-dozen carcasses swing from the rail of the back doors, sweeping an arc of blood as they travel. The children follow, waving their sticks and bones. Flames lift in the breeze, then die in the stillness, the urchins' yells just audible above the rumble of the engine.

In no time Charlie and Charlotte set up camp. Charlie sets about the animals that have painted a bloody arc on the back doors, Charlotte lent her heft. Soon half a dozen skins carpet the ground. Charlie butchers, Charlotte scrapes morsels of flesh from the skins. Respectful dogs wait, then squabble as she tosses out flaps of sinew and membrane. Darko sits at her side, Shady wanders the camp with the other children.

The sun is low, but light lingers enough for the skins to be cleaned and smeared with the brains of the same animals to preserve them. Charlotte tosses them up on top of the roof, out of reach from roaming dogs that she tossed the half-skulls to. Then she cranks the mincer handle and threads morsels of meat on sticks. They light a fire, burn it down to coals, warm the plate to a sizzle. Soon Black Charlie's is open for business, the biscuit tin is full, and just as soon, the little camp drifts away to other camps. Those of strong back and agile limb to work the orchards. Those of groaning backs and complaining limbs to do their laundry and start again.

49 Cherrystone Lane
— long ago

Memorial

At the corner of Cemetery Bridge and Cherrystone Lane is a rocket, two metres high, made from steel, set on a plinth of concrete. In front of the rocket is a single headstone dedicated to Daniel Duff and Michael Mugwort.

The original text reads:

Here rest the remains of

Daniel Duff

born May 21 1945 – deceased December 20 1958

Michael Mugwort

born April 1 1945 – deceased December 20 1958

Along with the neatly chiselled dedication are certain amendments and comments. Some are boldly evident and transcribable, others diluted, faded over time and the communal scouring of the obscene, or unacceptable.
Rockets were big and getting bigger in the fifties. This one may not be so big but as a prophesy it was mighty. Those that stumble upon it are mightily appreciative, as are the folk of the Lane.

Over time the legend of Danny and Michael has grown, spread, blossomed, and atrophied. Over time their headstone has reflected many truths and enhanced myths. Truth and myth are close, squabbling relatives in the story of family and community, and often interfere with each other.

Crudely inscribed, via continuous friction, with something like a screwdriver and less laboriously, but with more flourish, daubed with a can of spray paint, the headstone has received many amendments. It currently reads as follows:

Over there

Somewhere **Here rest the remains of**

Daniel Duff
born May 21 1945 – deceased December 20 1958
Michael Mugwort
born April 1 1945 – deceased December 20 1958

Complete Eejits

Danny and Michael worked in the orchard that was once the richest orchard country in the world. Where apples and cherries and other fruit made the most profit and were considered the sweetest fruit of any temptation.

Both lads got to work in the orchard because their mothers were good workers: picking, packing and grading. That was never said of Danny and Michael. Grades from the village school were mostly wanting, while teachers were often wanting to know the whereabouts of both. But smarts has little to do with school and as the smarter of the two Danny could always work out and remember when places were empty, when it was safe to sneak in and what was good to pilfer. As the less smart of the two Michael kept lookout and could always sniff out the best cider.

Now along with the sweetest fruit, that ripened as it travelled by the latest refrigerated boat to England, the cider brewed by the men and women folk of this valley was famous throughout the Apple Isle as the best and most potent cider to be had. While some barrels were loaded for the big city, the very best, and said to be psychedelic, was to be found tucked away in the darkest corners of orchard sheds and barns.

It was flagons of such that young Duff and Mugwort sought and indeed discovered at the back of the barn,

49

guarded by a wall of rockets, standing like sleeping sentries. These were the days after the second world war when rockets were plentiful and becoming increasingly popular and, in this case, used to dispel brooding hailstorms that could decimate a ripe cherry crop in minutes.

Sent to the clouds, said rockets would neutralise the threat of hail with a payload of silver iodide that, when exploded at altitude, would turn icy skin piercing pellets into less damaging, but still unwelcome rain.

Following a jar or two of special reserve cider Danny and Michael, settled back to contemplate the stack of slender projectiles and smoke a pilfered cigarette.

'How's about we shoot one out the door mate.'

'Ohhhhh yeeeeh,' or something like that, slurred Michael.

So they set one up, lit the fuse and it whooshed out the door, down the road and disappeared across the river.

'Maaaaate,' exclaimed young Danny, following its trail before it crashed somewhere on the eastern shore, 'let's ride em eh.'

'Yeeeeeeh, across the river.'

That's how the legend began. The next day Garrick Watt of the Messenger came to report on a couple of explosions near a couple of sleepy little villages along the Huon River with nothing more of a target than orchards, a scattering of orchard folk and a big shiny new apple shed.

Arriving first on the Eastern shore Garrick deduced it must have come from one of two places: across the river, or across the world. To the other shore in a chugging old boat, of swept stern and clanking engine, that traded up and down the river, the journalist steamed. There he came upon a crowd, milling around the burned remains of a building and deduced that he might have found ground zero.

Garrick began to make notes, describing a solemn crowd poking the ashes with heavy boots and sticks. The mood broken by an angry orchardist, peering at the debris and then to the sky, was inflamed by two ranting women looking for their boys. At first none understood the ranting, then Archie James of the orchard, on his way home in a grump at the loss of his shed and its contents, toed over a charcoaled boulder and a set of teeth grinned back at him.

Heads craned, the young stooped and gawped at the ashes and detritus. The women, almost as one, clasped handkerchiefs poised in readiness. Only Ivy, The Chinese, as she was known to most, stood apart, as she always did. The old men gaped corpse jawed, barely a breeze of breath, then arranged themselves and others into two close lines an arm length apart. Ivy joined her husband and his sister. The young remained around the edges.

Led by the expressionless men they scoured the site. With nothing to mark their gruesome finds individuals sheered from the lines. Soon a ragged map of the boys' last resting places was plotted and two lines of 10 and 11 adults became one line of five. And so the future shape of Memorial Park was plotted.

Watts made a note: two victims. Next was to discover a motive.

'Target,' espoused by old Wally Bones, a dab hand in the orchard, but gibbering drunkard when not. 'Coldstore,' he mumbled, 'they's went for that new fridgerated shed.'

'It's over,' nagged Wally's wife.

'What,' slurred Wally.

'The war, you daft old man.'

Just then little May piped up from her mother's knee, 'I've got a cold sore.' All prim and proud she pulled out her bottom lip let it go then asked, 'where's Danny, Mum?'

The little girl peered up at her mother then down at the charcoal remains as a squall cut across the ashes, worrying embers to life. The little girl twisted her face from the smoke, the old men cast a glance up at the sky in scrutiny of the clouds.

Garrick thanked the little girl for showing him her lip and moved through the crowd.

'There's no gold here,' muttered another of the old men, standing at attention, next to a solitary arm, 'never has been. My old man and me panned the whole rivulet, from the pines to the flats, not a skerrick.'

'What,' asked Watt, picking his way across the ashes and body parts.

'No gold, so no law,' the old man summarised.

'What,' repeated Watt, getting closer.

'No gold, so no gold law,' repeated the old man, at increased volume.

'Old war,' spoke another old man, also standing to attention next to a ragged body part, a flagon of cider dangling from his left hand, 'we was in the old war, me and Bob.'

'Yes, we was,' confirmed Bob.

'What,' cried Watt.

'Old war,' chanted the two old men, passing the flagon.

'Oh that.' Watt caught the inflexion of what they were telling him, 'Yes me too.'

'What,' called the old men.

So it was that the conflict to mark the remainder of an already conflict filled century was christened when Garrick Watt of The Messenger posted his story from the telephone at the school.

Cold War Bombing

in Huon Valley

The following weekend the site of the explosion was visited by a steady stream of sightseers from the city to the north. Mostly young, mostly in their parent's cars, mostly ghouls, they came to witness the site of the cold war rocket launching, scratching around for a souvenir, before seeking cider.

As the crowd grew the locals of the Lane set about roping off the site and demanding some respect for the poor lads that had perished. And that's how Cold War Park, or Rocket Park, as it's become known, was established.

The next weekend the heavens cracked and the ripe cherries were smashed, for the valley had no rockets to defend itself against the hail. The harvest failed, orchardists failed, Cold War Park and the memory of Danny and Michael was cursed in the breath of all but the closest of relatives. Only the ingenuity of Bob and his mate and a couple of other old men and their approximation of a sweet cherry flavoured spirit they'd sampled during the old war, saved the village.

Today, as I cast my eye to the park, a visitor is leaving and another pulls in. While it is not the grave of a famous rock star, author, or revolutionary, it is sacred ground, nicely managed by the local Landcare troop, its lawn maintained by a gaggle of geese. A convenient flat spot to park for a few nights, popular with fruit pickers in their campervans, station wagons and little tents that, in the summer, crowd right up to the rocket.

84 Cherrystone Lane
— recently

Sleep Well

When half the world was no longer painted pink no one wanted apples from the Apple Isle and a lot of trees were grubbed out and replaced with cattle for the nation's barbecues. That's when Roy and Linda bought part of an old orchard, at the head of Cherrystone Lane. It stretches from lush summer meadow, shared with black swans that raise their young in the marsh, to wooded hills of wattle, eucalyptus, and rough pasture.

Roy and Linda came first to Tasmania on a romantic whim, spent two weeks exploring the rivers and lakes of the high western mountains, before properly falling in love and falling in love with the Huon Valley. Neither Roy or Linda knows which came first and both seemed to love each other and the valley equally. To look at them both they are your average couple, of average height, build and intelligence. She always said they were 'solid', individually and together. There was nothing that Linda couldn't describe as 'solid'. Even the rivulet, in all its liquid fervour, was solid in its constancy and supply.

When the opportunity came to buy good acreage, with unlimited water from the rivulet, they begged and borrowed, scrimped and saved and soon filled the old farmhouse with five daughters, solid daughters, even the waif like last. Over five successive years they filled the fields with five cows, solid cows, despite their bony hips and ribby sides, sacrificed for the production of enough milk to bathe the children in.

While most were fattening cattle for beef Roy was a dairyman from the south coast of New South Wales, where the pastures led to rich milk, butter, cream, and cheese. So each of Roy's cows gave bloom to the rosy cheeks of his five daughters, growing most of them strong and round. Any leftover milk fed the dogs they kept to help round up the cattle, growing them solid, then the children of the neighbourhood.

When not moving the cattle between paddocks and fetching them in for milking, Roy and Linda turned their hands to other tasks and casual and seasonal work that came their way. By the time the girls had swollen the intake of the village school Roy and Linda had become valuable members of the little community and found time to explore the river, that the rivulet tumbled into, in the canvas canoe in which their partnership first blossomed.

As the girls grew Linda kept them close and schooled them in the ways of womanhood and warned them of the ways of the local lads. Together Roy and Linda told them stories of the world beyond their island, of the wonders of the big island to the north, and of far off lands, where things were more different still. They encouraged them to discover such wonders for themselves but not to forget where they came from.

Each daughter listened well. Over the course of another five consecutive years Roy and Linda found themselves as two again and had no need for the cows. So they turned the paddocks over to sheep, of bald faces and black feet, that thrived on marshy land. From their fleeces they gathered wool, spun and weaved and made articles of tiny clothing in expectation.

Within a further five years, one by one, the daughters returned, wiser, smarter, skilled, and rich with knowledge of different ways to be. Two trailed with them men that quickly gained the approval of Roy and Linda. One came with a man whose embrace within the family was slower to set, but came to be understood. A fourth fetched a man that did not take and wandered away. Soon that daughter found her way to her first love, a shining nugget among the local lads she was previously warned from. The last returned empty but with a yearning for a lass across the river, that Roy and Linda grew aware of but left space for her to speak her truth when she chose to.

As the tiny clothes they'd made in expectation began to be worn, grown out of and handed down, Roy began to fade. It was first noticed when a toddler informed Grandma that Grandpa was asleep at the loom. A day or two later, Linda found him asleep in the garden, where he was digging potatoes, then he simply faded into the same potatoes at the dinner table.

Upon being woken, by vigorous shaking of his limbs and slapping his face, Roy had no idea where he was, or who it was slapping him. Soon everyone he met was a stranger and needed to introduce themselves, over and over again. Soon Roy became rankled at being woken and lashed out with a fist strengthened around a cow's udder.

'Let me sleep. Why did you wake me?'

Linda and daughters came to wear the marks of waking him. Only Tinker the last working dog was quick enough to escape the old man's fist. Increasingly waking to the face of strangers, Roy would moan, 'let me sleep,' lashing out at whoever stood over him, 'I'm just sleeping.'

Neighbours too found him along the road, slumped in the hedgerow while out walking and most folk, apart from the reserved family in the big manor house and the sullen young women from the end of the road, also came to wear the bruises of Roy's fists.

One old man wheeling his wife along the road had to disentangle Roy from roadkill wallaby, where it was difficult to tell where the blood from the mangled wallaby ended and the blood leaking from Roy's head began.

'Leave me alone,' and, with the grip of a dairyman, he grabbed the man by his braided beard, 'I just want to sleep,' pulled him close and split his nose. A third pool of blood spilled onto the road.

At the annual family birthday party, when all the girls, born within a week of each other in successive years, celebrated their birthdays together Roy was working on his old canoe. He was becoming harder to wake and his violent outbursts upon being woken were more rage-full. The youngest grandchild was sent to find him and returned tearful, hands over his face, to report Grandpa had nodded off again, woken then gone back to sleep. The family glanced around the table and noted a resemblance, not genetic but born out of proximity and goodwill. Turning to each other in the same direction, indicated by the bend of their collective snouts, mindful that yet another child would miss some time at school, time to heal, they decided that enough was enough.

Together they carried the laden canoe to the river's edge, where a gaudy gaggle of plastic kayaks rested. For while paddling had become a family affair, none could be bothered with the constant repair that Roy dedicated to his and opted for vibrant easy care robust vessels. Gathering pebbles from the mud and dry grass and twigs from the shore they tied a faggot of kindling and set it in the bow of Roy's boat. Towing the old canvas craft out into the river, they lit the bundle of kindling and watched as the lighted wood flared embers into the boat igniting the oiled canvas and tinder dry frame.

'Sleep well father dear, sleep well,' they spoke solemnly beneath the starry night as it gathered a green and purple hue, 'dear father, sleep well.'

As the weighted bow tipped into the dark water, Linda raised a hand to wave farewell to the man she'd shared a lifetime with. 'Sleep well my love.' She cast her wish with tears and a kiss across the water and Roy raised a fist in return.

It was late before the lights went back on at Roy and Linda's place. The sky retained the same green and purple throb that framed my eye. I looked out to the river and wondered what it would be like to paint the same face every day.

75 Cherrystone Lane
— anytime

Scary Pete

Scary Pete scared the children. They were used to beards that cast a smooth shadow on the faces of young men, like their fathers, were grandfatherly full, or conjured the image Father Christmas. But not long and braided into three stiff skeins of rat grey.

A small man, Scary was light in movement but strong of arm. The result of shunting boxes of vegetables around most of his life. To Scary his work was a means to an end. Work he never took home, except for the odd sack of potatoes or bunch of carrots. Work that simply enabled him to maintain a number of wives.

In the Huon Valley, at the bottom of the world, winter is harsh. Scary doesn't like winter. Most of all Scary hates the fog that lingers over the rivulet, breathes down the back of his neck and whistles into his plumber's crack.

After his first winter Scary kept his shirt tucked in, sleeves rolled down and collar buttoned up. So that only the tip of, what looked like, two thick black snake heads poked out either side of his neck. He even kept his trousers tucked into his socks, should the fog gather an upward draft.

Scary has the property on the flat side of the 'creek', where, in spring, it runs fast and churns up a dirty white foam that gets snagged between rocks and roots and fallen trees. He calls it a creek, despite being told by all the neighbours it's a rivulet.

'It looks like a creek,' he'd reply, 'and we'd call it a creek where I come from too.'

There is a little house on the property. Four rooms of equal size set in a square beneath a pitched roof of faded red iron. There is a veranda, front and back and a couple of big sheds on the edge of a small paddock. The sheds are in disrepair but standing strong and good to house a tractor, that Scary admits is oversized for his five acres but sounds lovely, and that he'd kind of fallen in love with at first grunt.

Most days he uses his tractor to fix fences, pull trees out of the creek, and move heavy stuff around, which he likes to do often. At the end of the day, he drives the hulking white machine slowly into the shed, sits on it for as long as it takes to roll and smoke a cigarette, listens to its diesel clank, turns it off and covers it with a heavy dust sheet.

The house is in a slightly better condition. Scary soon makes it more comfortable by extending out under the back veranda, as most folk do in these parts, to make an eat-in kitchen and a bathroom, that can fit more than a dunny, a rotting shower and concrete laundry trough. He fixes up the front of the house too, so it is a nice place to watch the creek flow by and gives a good line of sight and distance to lob his empty tinnies into the back of his ute.

He brought two wives with him that live in each of the bedrooms while Scary lives in the front room that would have otherwise been the lounge. Every weekend he takes one of his wives out, but only if the weather is good. He cares for them both equally and fears for them in the rain, which also means he has to dry them off when they get home. Mostly they go out in the summer when it's hot and dry and Scary can roll his sleeves up and unbutton his collar. Or, when it is really hot, dispense with his shirt altogether. That's when Scary is at his most scary.

While he is diminutive in stature and much smaller than all the other men along the rivulet/creek, and some of the women, Scary wears the ink of a nightclub bouncer, or outlaw gang chief. As he wheels one his wives down his drive to the Lane that runs along the rivulet, mums and dads usher their children inside and older folk shake their heads in a tutting, 'what has become of the neighbourhood,' tremor.

On the weekend that he takes one wife out Scary spends the evening with the other. After dinner he slips into her room with a nice cold tinny, cuddles up to her, caresses her curves, her smooth shiny skin and strokes her forcefully down one side. She responds with a coughing grunt and low growl and he feels the throb of her heart. He works her from his wrist and her low growl rises and falls. Scary rises and falls then presses her button and silence falls, leaving only a foggy blue aroma of pleasure, that he breathes in deeply. He then rubs the side of his neck, where his wife's name is written in thick black swirling ink, dismounts, pulls a sheet back over her and tucks her in.

69 Cherrystone Lane

— tomorrow

Gobbledygook

Most of the year the Manor is hidden, tucked away behind tall European trees: oak, sycamore, chestnut and horse chestnut. There are also spruce and yew that reach above the spreading deciduous and add to the kaleidoscope of colour, that bursts as an autumn beacon along Cherrystone Lane. Beneath nature's grandness is a house of similar grand proportions. Built in a time of grand ideas, fuelled by a singular focus on the olde country, that supplied an equally grand income from the orchard that surrounds it.

A roof of many points and planes is exposed in winter, as the one and a half acre grounds become a slush of leaves, beneath skeletal trees. A wide wrap-around veranda, in a style common to pastoral stations on the big island to the north where the sun burns hot most of the year, shelters its inhabitants from rain and is just visible. Beneath it wide French windows, of uneven world wobbling glass, gaze southwest, across regimented rows of annually pruned fruit trees that once fed the house, those nearby and those far away.

Here now live the Bears. Mummy Bear, Daddy Bear, Little Bear and Baby Bear. Baby is not a baby but an inquisitive five-year-old while Little is an opinionated six-and-a-half-year-old. The Bears bought the Manor in Spring, on a gorgeous sunny day at the end of October. Mummy Bear couldn't believe how beautiful it all looked, new buds, new leaves, a honeyed heavenly scent, and a bigger house than both her sister and brother.

'It is as if God has delivered a piece of heaven to us,' spoke Daddy Bear, 'and surrounded it with mana.'

Mummy Bear looked at Daddy Bear, with big bear eyes and Little and Baby Bear jumped and pulled at Mummy Bear's clothing, 'please, please, please.' Then a ray of golden sunshine haloed them all and Mummy Bear spoke, 'I think we are blessed,' and she smiled radiantly, the straightest, purest of smiles, at Daddy Bear.

'I think so too my love.'

A month later the Bears made it their home and hung a sign at the gate *The Bears - Blessed by God*. The mana had fallen to earth and shiny new leaves and tiny fruit had grown in its place. Soon they were decorating for Christmas. It would be a very special Christmas this year, in a very special house.

Each day during the week Mummy and Daddy Bear take Little and Baby Bear to a place where they learn to add up and spell, get on with other children and pray. This means that Mummy Bear and Daddy Bear can earn lots of money to pay for the Manor.

During those days Mummy Bear stays with Little and Baby Bear and teaches older children to spell. Daddy Bear goes to another building where he fixes people's smiles. At the end of the day Mummy Bear takes Little and Baby Bear to get Daddy Bear. Sometimes they have to wait in the car while Daddy Bear finishes fixing smiles, making teeth straight and pearly white.

Mummy Bear says, 'straight and pearly white is beautiful. The image of god, and a smile like Jesus.' Then they drive home where Mummy Bear takes something out of a big white metal box and heats it in a little white metal box that goes ping. They say a little prayer, eat everything that is in front of them and are grateful.

On the first day of the weekend Little and Baby Bear play in the garden. They start by running around the veranda.

Soon they spiral out, racing and hiding among the big trees and bushes, stopping only at the picket fence that separates the garden from the big orchard.

On the second day of the weekend, that is really the first day of the next week, all the Bears rise early and drive to another big house with a pointy roof. There they listen to a man in black, eat biscuits and sing and pray. After that Little Bear and Baby Bear go to a room with other children to listen to stories and draw pictures. Baby Bear's favourite story is about a donkey, which she'd like to keep in the garden, while Little Bear likes the one about a nice looking man on a cross who looks a bit sad but has a beautiful smile and another one with a man in it who doesn't look quite right, because he has a crooked face and crooked smile, with bumps on his head and face. They draw pictures of donkeys and handsome men but are not allowed to draw crooked men.

Soon the last window on the advent calendar is open. As are the windows of the house to try and let in a cooling breeze. The big tree in the big lounge room is hung with shiny red baubles, as are the little stumpy trees in the orchard and Little and Baby Bear have hung up their stockings and are sent out to play while the big Bears wrap up presents.

Just as the last present is wrapped and hidden away Baby Bear bursts in screaming.

'Mummy Mummy I saw a devil.'

'It's true, it's true,' follows up Little Bear, 'they're in the orchard, everywhere.'

'Don't be silly now girls,' comforts Daddy Bear, 'they only come out at night and there aren't many of them. And you know they're not really devils.'

'No Daddy, it's true, there are lots of them and they make gobbledygook noise. Like the lady at church that fell down,' panted Little Bear in that stubborn six-and-a-half-year-old way.

'You mean Mrs Cabrito,' interrupts Mummy Bear with a soothing tone. 'It's called speaking in tongues, it's what happens when god enters you and is very special.'

'No Mummy,' the girls chime insistently.

The big Bears glance at each other with a sense of something serious. Mummy Bear clasps her crucifix. Little Bear continues, 'they speak to each other in gobbledygook and one said gobbledygook to Baby.

'Gobbledygook gobbledygook gobbledygook,' Baby chants.

Mummy Bear draws them both close. 'You've had a fright, probably the shadows. Now let's get you some milk and something to eat. Then we'll go and find your devils.'

The girls, comforted by the thought of food, follow Mummy Bear into the kitchen at the corner of the house, where she pulls two slices of bread from a bag and spreads them with something from a tub and something red from a jar. Just as Little Bear and Baby Bear chew into their sandwiches a strange language drifts in on the cooling breeze. Little and Baby Bear, sandwiches in their mouths, look up at Mummy Bear in a plea for safety and a little bit— we told you so.

'Daddy Bear, come quick,' and so he does. 'Listen.'

Together they listen to the noise that enters the house. Little Bear looks up, 'see,' and together Little and Baby Bear whisper, 'gobbledygook.'

Together the family approach the back door and led by the incomprehensible chatter tiptoe cautiously through the garden to the picket fence, where they come to a gang of young people picking cherries, singing and chattering as they pick.

'See,' the girls say loudly, tucked behind Mummy Bear, 'and they're picking all the pretty red balls off the trees.'

Just then the picker nearest, a lithe, dark skinned, young man, turns, sweeping a curtain of dreadlocks aside, he smiles a gap-toothed smile of crooked teeth that lifts three small uniform scars on the left side of his face.

'See, a devil,' cry Little and Baby Bear, gripping Mummy Bear tighter.

'They're just people. People from another place. They come to pick the fruit and then go home. There is nothing to worry about girls.'

The picker with the smile leant a long sinewy arm across the picket fence. Little and Baby retreated behind their mother. In two slender fingers he held two perfectly formed cherries connected at the stem, the sun catching their glossy redness. Little and Baby retreated further as the picker spoke three words of English with a confidence that suggested there were more.

'For the children.'

'Thank you,' said Daddy Bear. Little and Baby tugging at their mother in the direction of the house and as one they retreat to the security of the Manor.

'Daddy, they have crooked smiles. Can you fix them?' Pleads Baby Bear in confused retreat.

'It's not that simple,' he begins, offering the cherries to the children, 'you have to work hard to get money to get fixed.'

'But they are working hard Daddy. Can you please fix them, please,' begs Little Bear.

'Yes, they are working hard but they need to want to be fixed. They need to want to spend their money on getting fixed.'

'But Daddy,' continues Little Bear, 'if you don't fix them and Santa sees them, he will think we've been bad with all the devils around and won't leave any presents and...and' she fades as her breath fades, as Daddy Bear offers them the gifted cherries.

'I don't like them,' concludes Baby Bear and Mummy Bear looks at Daddy Bear in silent agreement.

That night as the gobbledegook fell silent and the pickers retreated to their huts and tents, the Bears lock all the doors, say a prayer and Big and Little go to bed. As confused as they were in the afternoon they lay awake as long as they can, listening for Santa. Just as they begin to doze off a deep throaty, mechanical roar, from the little cottage across the way, down by the rivulet, rattles the air and Little and Baby close their eyes tight in the hope Santa is near.

89 Cherrystone Lane
– last week

Hole in one

Between the rivulet and the Lane, lower than the Lane, sometimes lower than the rivulet, is a patch of land, that only a person brought up below sea level, or versed in the stories of such a people, could love.

Built on this threatened block is a high standing house, set on piers, tall enough to drive a small car under. There are two vehicles parked beneath the house and one outside. The two beneath the house rarely leave.

In the house live a man and his mother. She is old, so old she has mostly reverted to her first language and other habits learned in the country of her birth where she grew up. Her driving has become less predictable and less safe of late. She has knocked down the gate post a number of times, caused alarm when driving on the wrong side of the road and parked in the rivulet many times. Silly old duck nearly ran me off the road once coming along the lane on the wrong side. I stopped. She kept coming before turning into her drive, cursing me with a mouthful that sounded like she was hacking something up from deep down. It's probably best for everyone that we are both off the road now.

Sometimes she argues, with the same guttural hack, that the rivulet was not there when she parked. Sometimes she is right. So her son had a wall built from sandstone blocks, that cost $500 each, to keep his mother in and the rivulet out.

Fiete is also high standing, set on piers, as are many of the people in the land where he was born, but did not grow up. Two meters exactly. More in his pomp. Skinny as the club he carries around, he is still blond at sixty-six.

Most Tuesdays he takes his mother to the local community centre. While she plays whist or rummy at the centre, he pops down the road to play golf. When she's at home he practices his swing in the garden. Most of the time he swings at fresh air, sometimes plastic balls with holes in them. Other times he chips a hard little ball the length of his garden, aiming at a couple of old saucepans.

His garden is just over twice the length of the house. There is a water hazard on three sides. If he clears the rivulet, he is in the neighbour's paddock. There used to be one and a half acres of land to chip around. Since the rains of the last few Springs there is only one acre.

When he is not practicing his swing, chip, or putting into saucepans, he cleans the cars and looks after his mother. He is gentle, kind, and attentive. So gentle and kind he speaks to his little balls nicely, addressing them with a whispered blessing, before whacking them as hard as he can.

Across the rivulet, uphill from the paddock, is a white house. Before Daryl and Dolly moved in there used to be black cattle and white sheep in the paddock that rose up into the bush, that's been pushed back into the hills. Every year the family with the cows and sheep would slaughter some of their stock to fill the freezer. What they couldn't fit in the freezer they sold to neighbours along the road. Then they got old and moved to Queensland for the sunshine and to be with their grandchildren. Daryl and Dolly fatten only children. Two chubby boys that, after school and on weekends, ride highly strung motorbikes around the paddock, that sound like deeply irritated insects.

Fiete doesn't like the motorbikes. His mum doesn't like the noise, but doesn't know what is making it. After a week of banging her ears, with her head tilted to one side, trying to shake out the bee that she thinks is stuck between her ears,

Fiete took her to the window and showed her where the noise was coming from. Fiete's mother cursed in an archaic and regional language, that not even other migrants from her country understood very well, and asked him to speak to the neighbour.

After practice Fiete forded the rivulet to the paddock, steadying himself with his favourite nine iron, on the pretext of looking for a lost ball. The boys on their motor bikes alerted their dad. He came out the house with a smile and set of earmuffs. Fiete introduced himself and extended a hand. He was greeted not with a warm shake but with a set of earmuffs thrust into his open palm. 'Keep 'em mate,' said the man, 'I get them from work. I'm in the quarry. Now what sort of name is Fiete?'

'It means peace where I come from. It's Dutch.' Fiete thought about explaining that it wasn't really Dutch but Frisian, then recalling the puzzled looks he got in the office and crap he got at school thought better of it.

'Dutchy are yer? I'm Daryl. Got no idea what it means. It's from 'ere.'

Fiete glanced at the earmuffs in his hand, rested his club against his leg, tried them on, shook his head and took them off.

'I'm not sure mother will like them,' he said, handing them back, 'besides I can still hear the motor bikes.'

'That's cos you're outside mate,' Daryl grinned and handed them back, 'when you're inside they work a treat, go on.'

Fiete declined, 'I still don't think mother will like them. So could your boys just ride a few days, do you think?'

'Nah mate, not gonna to happen. State championships coming up.' Daryl lit a cigarette from pack of fifty.

'Oh, I see. And after that will they stop?'

'Not likely. It's in their blood, they got talent and yer can't get in the way of that, can yer.'

'I see.'

Fiete reported the visit to his mother. She thanked him for trying and Fiete went to practice in the garden. Later, he made dinner. Dumplings and stretchy cheese sauce.

'You still make the dumpling good son.' She said in her enduring Frisian.

'Thanks, but it's getting more difficult to get the cheese. I have to go further. It's not like when you got milk from just down the road and made your own cheese, and you know I could never master that,' he replied in perfect English.

Mother listened, without really listening, then instructed, 'Tomorrow, when the boys are not home you should go and you should talk with him again. Okay?' she said, concentrating on the words of an increasingly distant language.

Fiete nodded, finished his dumplings, cleared the table, and washed up. Then he went to practice in the garden. First, he whipped the air with a sweeping swoosh, then he took a box of balls from the back of his car, set them, one by one, on a tee and addressed them kindly, raising his club back and bringing it forward to a fraction before the ball. He repeated the action a few times, with a stiff clock like spring of the club in both directions, then struck each ball with a powerful arc of release.

The next morning, he picked his way across the rivulet, again using his club to steady himself on the stones. He loped across the paddock and up the drive and knocked on Daryl's door. A small dog yapped a high-pitched bark from within the house, then footsteps came clonking to the door. The door opened and a sleepy Daryl, in tracky-dackies, tyre company t-shirt and soft indestructible shoes, grumped a greeting, popped his cigarette into his mouth and extended his hand. 'Fiete,' he mispronounced.

'I seem to have over hit some of my balls into your paddock.' Daryl scratched his own and grunted acknowledgment. Fiete continued, 'Do you mind if I look for them?'

'Knock yerself out mate,' replied Daryl with surprising vigour.

Fiete collected nearly two dozen balls. One he could not find. He went back to the house to thank Daryl, who he found washed and dressed.

'Thank you,' said Fiete, 'I found all but one. I surprised myself how far I hit some of them.'

'No worries,' said Daryl, 'you really do love your golf don't yer.'

'I do. I've been playing for many years. It's a relaxing game and oddly enough keeps you quite fit.' Fiete demonstrated the stretching of different muscles through his swing in stop motion. Daryl watched with mild interest.

'Now while I'm here can we talk about the noise from the motorbikes. Is there anywhere else they can practice?' Fiete stood back from the door and took a practice swing at an imaginary ball. As he stood, with his club wound back over his shoulder, he noticed a small white ball in the flower bed. 'Oh, look there it is. Now that's quite a way isn't it.'

'From your place, with that stick, bloody oath.'

Fiete took another practice swing, 'I wonder,' then placed the lost ball on the ground in front of him, set himself and whispered a polite address. Daryl leaned in to catch what Fiete was saying. Fiete swung. The ball took off with a swoosh. Fiete followed its trajectory as it took off flat and low then rose into the air dropping just before the rivulet and rolled to its edge. Daryl was visibly impressed.

Fiete turned, 'now about the noise.'

'Boys are boys,' said Daryl, stepping back, 'got to keep 'em sweet or they're hell to live with.'

'Yes, I have a mother the same and those bikes are driving her mad, which is driving me mad.' He placed another ball on the ground in front of him, addressed it. Daryl leaned in to try and catch what Fiete was saying. Fiete wound his club back, held it, took a practice stroke then struck the ball. It landed in the creek. 'Hell to live with,' he repeated to Daryl, who by now was somewhat impressed by the power of Fiete's swing. 'Yes, it can bring out the worse in you, can't it, if someone is forever nagging.'

'She's old mate, just ignore 'er,' Daryl lit another smoke, 'or stick her in a home. More time for golf then. Got to look after yourself mate,' he concluded with a wide grin.

Fiete placed another ball on the ground, addressed it. Daryl leaned in closer to listen. Fiete took a practice swing, moved close, wound back, cocked his swing, and swung hard. The ball took off, bounced twice and the third time skipped over the rivulet, made a little hop, then clanked into a pot. Fiete looked on in great satisfaction, before turning to address Daryl.

'Now about the noise.'

Daryl was hunched and wheezed, his smoke laying on the ground in front of him. He tried to straighten up but couldn't. He raised his head slightly, coughed, then squealed a yap that set off the little dog and quickly hunched back, chest on his knees, one hand steadying him in his squat, the other searching between his legs, taking in deep gasping breaths that made him squeal more. He began to pant, blowing out more air than he took in.

'You will hyperventilate if you keep that up,' Fiete advised. 'Sorry about that. I should have warned you to keep your distance. My friends say I have a ferocious wind up.'

Daryl winced upward, blew out two sharp breaths, followed by two constrained wheezes like a wounded accordion and addressed Fiete, who loomed high above, 'I think, huh...huh... huh... you've busted one,' he almost whispered, still fishing around between his legs.

'Sorry, I didn't catch that. Must be going deaf in my old age.'

'I think you've smashed... huh.. huh... wheeze... huh... huh... wheeze, one of my balls, huh... huh... wheeze, it's not there.' Daryl coughed involuntarily, let out a shrill groan that started the little dog again and continued fishing.

'I'll,' two more outward breaths, 'talk to them.'

'Thank you. Mother will be pleased, and of course she will be more easy to live with. Now I must gather my balls.'

193 Cherrystone Lane
— the other day

Birds, Nasty, Smelly, Noisy Birds

The hairdresser had just left. She gazed into the mirror one more time. She knew she looked good. Her burgundy-black revived, the grieving grey banished for another month at least.

Her hair hangs in loose curls past her shoulders, winding country roads trailing to her shining cleavage. Once again, she looks like the movie star her mother named her after. Her scent is heavy with confidence, enough to go door-to-door and meet the neighbours, introduce herself and get to the bottom of those nasty, smelly, noisy birds that disturb her beauty sleep.

She inches her sausage link legs into her skintight black jeans, stretching them up over her pudding belly and ballasting butt. They hug every curve, highlight every crevice. Her overlong cardigan will act like a body veil, allowing her to flaunt or not, while at the same time offering a comfort blanket of retreat.

She passes her gumboots, flopping them out of her path. Less practical for such an adventure she slips into her tan ankle boots, zip and pointy toe, with a nub of a heel. Sophia is never out without heels, even her overlooked gumboots have a rubbery rise.

She drives her shiny little retro styled sports car downhill for 100 meters, takes an almost hairpin right at the bridge that crosses the rivulet then slowly, very slowly, along the middle of the dirt road. Sophia doesn't like dirt and fears gutters, so naturally gravitates to the middle of narrow roads. Getting out of the car she shivers beneath the great Macrocarpa pines that hide the sun. Gingerly she walks around two sides of the house before spotting the front door. 'It's much easier in the city, where front doors are at the front,' she curses, then knocks loudly. No answer. She knocks again. She hears footsteps and waits.

'Step back from the door,' orders a woman's voice from the other side. The door bursts open with a rush. Sophia catches its draft.

'It sticks sometimes,' explains the woman in the doorway.

Sophia introduces herself and explains that she and her husband have just moved in across the road, then cuts straight to the point. 'We were wondering if you knew anything about the birds?'

'Birds?' the woman in the doorway repeats, twitching her mouth to one side then the other. 'No, we've just the birds in the trees. Pretty things if you can spot them. Robins, they're nice, lovely flash of red against the deep green. Oh, and we have fairies in up the back, little blue ones about the size of the robins, but with bright blue caps. Lovely little wrens, I think.'

'No, the noisy birds, the one's that keep me awake. Big ones.'

'Oh, the cockatoos. They are a bit noisy, but they don't stay long. Did you know there are stories about them bringing rain, but I can't remember how it goes. Now you'll have to excuse me I've a bit of a flood to see to,' and she closes the door, gently at first, then opens it and heaves it hard to seat it squarely in its less than square frame.

Next stop. The house back the way she came, just across the bridge. She parks on the road, staying well clear of the wide gutter, an unidentifiable carcass trapped at the culvert. She cautiously picks her way up the short drive, skirting puddles and little mounds of chicken shit. She climbs three easy steps to the wooden deck, her heels clicking in authoritative tenor. She taps on the glass door. Again, a woman answers. She introduces herself and, like before, doesn't listen to the women in the doorway before asking about the birds.

'Nah, got chooks, but they're not that noisy. Even Randy, that's the rooster. He's a quiet one. Was yer after chooks? I see's yer's just moved in. You'll be wanting good layers. I've none to spare myself but I'll keep an ear out.'

'No no, no, I don't think we'll be keeping,' she searched, 'chookens.'

'Thank you,' Sophia adds in the motion of turning and is about to leave when the woman in the doorway calls her back.

'Here yer go luv, take some eggs with yer. We've got plenty. They might be a bit pooey, but yer won't get fresher.'

Sophia gathers a dozen eggs and tiptoes back to her car. A couple of black hens escort her, until distracted at the culvert.

She next stops at the pretty little cottage across the road where the rivulet tinkles past with fairy tale charm. The front door is open. An overfed cattle dog patrols the yard, behind a wire mesh fence. 'Hello,' she calls from the safe side of the fence.

Only the dog replies. She calls out again, louder, hoping to overcome the dog's bark and the rumble of an engine from inside the house. The machinery noise ceases. A small man, with a feral beard, eventually pads his way to the door, slips some thongs on, over his socked feet and continues to the gate to receive Sophia's introduction and hastily followed inquiry. 'Nah luv, no noisy birds here, old Razor sees 'em off.

Baulked by the familiar address and Razor's continued presence, Sophia doesn't press on but the man does. 'If you mean the cockies, luv, they're native not much you can do about them. Just have to learn to live with 'em. But the white ones, now they're down from the mainland, proper blowins those bastards. Dunno if there's much you can do about 'em but.'

Sophia thinks about pressing on with her inquiry but the man sculls the last of his can, crushes it and tosses it past her, into the back of his ute. 'Try the bloke down the road. He knows his animals.'

The man in the next house does indeed know his animals and birds and is less familiar. But first he advises her to pull her car off the road and into his driveway. 'There are some idiots come through here, taking the back road to avoid police checks, and that bend is a bit blind.'

Sophia pulls off the road.

'Now birds, noisy birds you say, waking you up. Big ones. What sort of noise? Is it a caw caw caw?' He cups his hands over his mouth to make the bird call, 'like that.'

'No,' says Sophia, feeling she might be getting somewhere.

'More of a screech then,' he cups his big hands again to get the right tone, 'like that.'

'No,' she says again, sitting back, expecting another bird call offering.

'Tell me then.'

'Oh, I couldn't.'

He goads her, 'down here you have to help yourself a bit. It's only me here. Go on, give it ago. I won't tell.'

Encouraged she places a hand each side of her mouth, without touching, 'It's more of a,' Sophia juts her head forward and a brief gurgle rises from her throat then falls flat in her mouth.

'Turkey, sounds like a gobbler to me. Folks up the road used to have some, but I think they've only chooks now. Since Christmas last year. They come down here for a feed once in a while, they like my greens, the chooks too, gentle birds they are, even old Randy.'

'No, they're not turkeys, or chickens,' insists Sophia.

Ducks maybe, I know there used to be a gaggle in the rivulet. Funny birds, a bit noisy when they get together. Try again with the sound.'

Sophia strains her head forward, tensions her neck muscles and emits a deep sort of swallowed honk, a droplet of spittle almost escaping right at the end.

'Goose,' erupts the man, slapping his pudgy hand on his equally pudgy thigh, 'well done. Big beautiful white birds with frilly knickers. That'll be them.'

'That's it' says Sophia, recovering from her embarrassment, blotting her spittle with a handkerchief. Relieved she won't have to make any more bird noises she continues, 'Now do you know who's they are?'

'Oh no, they came down years ago, from further up the rivulet, where the road starts to go up hill, took to some of the paddocks and dams.'

Oh, that's a shame, only I'd like whoever owns them to keep them away from our place. They're terribly messy too, and I'm forever cleaning up my lawn and driveway.'

'Lawn, you say. Geese love lawns. Not that many folk grow lawns in the country, and if they do, they fence them. Don't understand it myself. The pademelons love lawns too.' The man thinks for a bit before advising that she speak to the fellow down the road on the low side. 'he's been here a long time too, feeds them too, he might be able to help you. If he can't try the orchard, they let them in during the winter to crop the grass and fertilise the trees.

Encouraged, Sophia thanks the man and ventures down the road and down almost into the rivulet, where a tall blond man, greets her with formal politeness.

'Oh, the geese, lovely aren't they? We feed them a bit. Mother loves their glottal tones. She says they remind her of home and market days in her village.'

Sophia looks visibly lost, as if the tall man is speaking a foreign language. The tall man detects her puzzlement explaining how language is his thing. Sophia continues to be lost and most of what the tall man is saying passes way over her new perm. That which lands simply glazes her powdered face to an undesired gloss.

He continues to provide examples of the tone he is talking about, using a number of different accents and languages to demonstrate a glottal stop. Sophia, follows, as far as wondering how a stop could make a noise.

'Oh, I wish they would stop waking me up,' she says, trying to ease her way from the tall man's continued lecture, which he then continues despite her interruption. She finally raises her voice to interject and bring an end to his rant. 'Do you own them? Are they yours?'

The tall man, a little affronted by the interruption, responds with a succinct 'no, we do not. We feed them sometimes. You might try the orchard,' and gestures for her to leave, as he might an interrupting student.

Across and down the road a bit, she knocks softly on the side door. A little old lady in dark mournful black answers the door. A little old tan mongrel squats at her heels.

'Don't worry about Tinker. He won't hurt you. He's got no teeth. Now you must be from along the Lane, where it starts going uphill. Is that right?'

Sophia opens her mouth to speak but the little old lady's breath and words fill the space between them before she can make a sound. Sometimes a look and the way your lips part is answer enough. Little old ladies know that, 'so how can I help?'

'Birds, geese, I am led to believe,' says Sophia, reaching for high ground through precise, what she perceives to be, posh diction. She has a feeling this woman is not to be messed with and might go on like the tall man.

She shakes her locks in false weariness. 'I'm trying to find the owner of the geese that seem to roam,' she pauses briefly, taking time feel a bit chuffed with her language and thinks about the tall man and all his fancy words, 'along the road, terrorising people and making a mess and waking me up.' She keeps rolling, fearful that if she stops the little old lady will start filling the space between them. 'Do you please know who owns them?' She trails off with a teenage whine, made deeper and more breathy with age and weight. The little old mongrel, behind the little old lady, steps forward and regurgitates on the threshold, then immediately cleans up.

The little old lady casts a glance at the dog. 'You sound like you could do with a cup of tea. Pop your shoes off and come in, the kettle's always on.'

Popping her shoes off means reducing her height by an old fashioned two inches, exposing her feet on a worn hardwood floor and stepping across the threshold that a little old mongrel has just chucked up on and mopped up. Both prove to be an issue for Sophia.

The little old lady spots her hesitation, 'is Tinker a problem? He sort of has the run of the place.'

'Oh no,' she lies, 'we had a poodle before we came here. But we didn't want fences so gave her away.'

'Oh, did you, really.'

The little old lady does not insist with the offer of tea. 'We've had her since she was a pup. Couldn't imagine giving her up. Tell you what try at the orchard down the way.'

Leaving the little old lady's place, Sophia, drives past walls of black net, stretching, like thick black stockings, across the valley. A muddied and foreboding sign at the beginning of a track into the funereal vales reads DON'T DIE and something more that is covered in mud. Sophia drives on.

She passes a steep muddy track on the other side of the road, that scares her in the same way the track beneath the obscuring veils does. She disturbs a mob of black ravens starting in on a relatively recent roadkill until coming to a patch of ragged and straggly trees, scruffy with the unruly growth of previous years.

Pulling into a ragged driveway leading to a ragged building, that she thinks more like a shed than a house, with its lack of windows and too many doors, she has come to the end of Cherrystone Lane. The freeway and river lay beyond.

Confronted with four identical doors she taps on the first and brushes imagined dirt off her knuckles. No answer. She taps on the next door. Brushes off her knuckles. No answer. Same at the next two. She turns and is heading back to her car when a door slams and a small, ragged man with disproportionately long limbs, tumbles from the dunny at the end of the shed. The only door she didn't knock on.

'Allo.'

She turns, then turns again, shortly reaching the security of her car.

'Sorry,' she says, barely audible, 'I was looking for the owner of the orchard. About the geese.'

'My brother. Not here anymore. Gone.'

'Will he be back?'

'Gone. Dead.'

'Sorry to hear that. I won't keep you.'

'Have to pack and find keep.'

'Thank you.' She says, again, only heard by herself, starts the car, turns, and takes off back the way she came. Shortly the Lane is blocked by a meandering gaggle of twenty odd big white birds. She slows. The geese keep going. She follows. Her frustration grows as she drives slowly behind the geese, that seem unconcerned about the sporty little car, and its noisy little horn, behind them.

At the bottom of my drive I almost trip, dragged by an almost runaway wheely bin. A second one drags me back to balance. My dressing gown flops open. I tie it up and pick up the knife that's clattered onto the road.

As I trundle across the road, ahead of me a flock of geese veer to the edge. I line up the bins and am returning across the road, just as a smart little sports car is speeding up to pass the geese. I step quickly to avoid it. It stops sharply. I glare and curse the driver of the stalled vehicle. She eases down the window.

'Sorry, sorry, sorry' she says, this time audible.

'There's no rush. It's Sunday after all. Apology accepted but take it easy in future.' I trail of with a few curses.

'Sorry,' she repeats and makes her excuse, 'I really am terribly sorry. It's just I'm a bit tired and very frustrated.'

I wander round to the side of the car to listen,

'I'm trying to find the owner of those,' she points ahead.

'Aren't they lovely with their frilly knickers. Sebastopols,' I tell her admiring their fluffy bums.

'Where would I find him?' she asks with renewed vigour.

'Find who?'

'The owner, this Sebastopol.'

I look away and back up the road concealing a smirk that I know is spreading across my face. 'Oh, let me think now,' I play the confused old man, 'he's in the orchard somewhere. A bit of a recluse. See all that black net, take one of the dirt tracks. He's in there somewhere.'

Like a peloton of belligerent cyclist, the geese are waddling back into the middle of the road. Together, we watch as their frilly bottoms disappear around the bend.

'They sort of migrate along the road at different times of the year, depends where the grass is best. Slow the traffic down too,' I smile, 'as you've noticed. You can shuffle them off the road if you get close enough on one side. How far are you going? Taking the back road, are you?

'No, not far,' she pauses, 'just up the road,' she trails off in resignation, 'up where it starts to go up hill.'

'Oh well, good luck. Might be a slow drive. Lucky you're not going far. Now did I see a fresh wallaby carcass back there.'

22 Cherrystone Lane
— next year

Cuddy

Cuddy lives in four rooms. A small window in each looking west, a tad small to squeak the average backside through. To go from one room to another Cuddy has to first go outside. Outside, facing south, is a thin crumbling path of cracked concrete. Moss sprouts between cracks, dusted with a confetti of pink paint, flaking from the weatherboards. An equally stingy stretch of rusty corrugated iron follows the rise of the skillion roof, lifting to the south. The last sheet curls up like a cowlick in a coerced fringe. To use the toilet Cuddy has to trudge the broken path, past the cowlick, to the long drop. Housed in a skinny, detached shed, it defies the fierce northerlies that rock it back and forth on its frail concrete anchors.

This was how they built picker's huts nearly three quarters of a century ago, when apples were gold and labour cheap. There is a fireplace in the first room and a red brick chimney outside, that after seventy odd years of marriage is leaning toward a separation.

This is the living room, it's a bit bigger than all the other rooms, that used to accommodate two bunks and space to stand between. Opposite the hearth is a small table, its scratched red Formica surface, lifting from the pitted chrome frame, is nailed down with a gun-metal clout. On the table is a plugin bench top stove, a brittle red plastic washing up bowl and various cutlery in a skating dance with a bustle of chipped crockery. Two matching chairs are tucked under the table. The foam on the seats has burst through the torn vinyl and crumbles, like stale biscuits, with each sitting. Under the tiny window a ratty couch, once old gold velour, flabby exhausted cushions, peeking out from under a frayed blue candle wick bedspread, bleaching in a gob of winter sunshine.

Next to the fireplace is a wooden framed armchair, the type once found in doctor's waiting rooms, when your doctor knew you by sight. The coil springs stretching across the seat sag and give easily. The cushion on top is as exhausted as the couch. As are most folk trying to get out of it.

There is a bed in the second room, wooden slats, and more knackered foam beneath a limpid sleeping bag. The third is kept locked. Elderly chickens and a possum nest in the fourth.

Cuddy moved in here when his mother died. He is the sort of man that raises the question of where folk like him, that have lived with their mother all their life, been mothered all their life, go when she dies.

It's been six years since she passed. Old age, nothing dramatic. She likely got to the point of exhaustion, from caring for Cuddy all her adult life, that she simply wanted a rest and asked for the machines and medicine that were keeping her alive to be stopped.

Cuddy wasn't a difficult child, but he had needs. From an early age he learned to do things that most others didn't because they were out with friends having a good time. In many ways he was better equipped to take care of himself than men his age, whose wives had come to their senses and walked out on them. Cuddy could make tea, open a tin, and boil an egg. He could also wash up and sweep. He cleaned the bathroom — although his mum always did it again after him— and while most boys his age were learning to drive, he was entrusted with the lawnmower.

The picker's huts, like the orchard and main house his brother lived in, have been in the family for generations. The house, the huts, and the trees in the orchard have been let go. They still give fruit. Heirloom and heritage fruit they call it now but in the old days they were simply apples, wrapped in tissue, packed in wooden crates, and labelled after the orchard they came from, usually the initials of the grower.

If the plaque on the wall at the little community museum, in the nearby village, is to be believed, this orchard was once part of the 'richest orchard country in the world, yielding more tonnage of fruit per acre than anywhere else.' Now its untamed bounty is unwanted and out of reach and many trees have succumbed to disease and rot.

Cuddy's bother didn't care for the orchard, or Cuddy for that matter. He let Cuddy have the picker's huts because they were out of the way, and on the proviso that he stayed out of the way and didn't embarrass him when he was occasionally home. His brother always found Cuddy an embarrassment. It was he that gave him the Cuddy moniker from which he's never been able to escape. Or rather it was his maternal grandfather, visiting from the far north of an equally cold, rainy, and windswept island, a whole world away, that fed the eldest boy the words with which to define his little brother just as he was about to start school. 'Yer wee softy cuddy, wee daft softy cuddy, softy cuddy,' he chanted that summer, and soon most of the boys and some of the girls at school joined him.

Through a difficult adolescence Cuddy grew to own the spiteful christening he'd undergone and gathered a reputation as a young man with a short fuse. As he grew into adulthood that fuse stretched and hardened to an occasional flare up if he felt taken advantage of. It is fair to say a retreat to the domestic environment and his mother's guiding hand reduced the incidence of an explosive temper.

While Cuddy's temperament grew to calmness, as he matured to adulthood, his physique remained that of a teenager. Sinewy limbs, thin and knobbly, like those of the trees that surrounded him now, never seemed to fit his stunted and chubby torso. Puppy fat lingered on a face that sprouted only tufts of downy bum fluff. Never bristling to whiskers.

Wrinkles also passed him by, without etching in their passing. At 60 the pathetically wispy mop, on his box square head, became as patchy as the rest of his hair. Youthful middle age, puffed with puppy fat, dusted to a flat velvet mat, coalesced in his smile and the easy movement of confident toddler.

Years back when I was first deserted, for Christ and then the convenience of the suburbs, I got him up to dig some holes. He was a strong man for all his oversized joints, knees like clenched boxing gloves, elbows like knees and wrists that showed no differentiation from his fists. He dug a good hole. At the end of every one he would tell me I needed a tractor.

I would have liked to have discussed with him how machines breakdown and need fuel that makes pollution and that in their making they make more pollution and sit around doing nothing most of the time. But instead, I told him if I had a tractor I wouldn't need him and we moved on to footy. He liked footy. He understood the game but had no team. Not even my crap team. He knew players and would mimic their moves, but he wore no colours. He knew the game well but had no tribe.

When his brother was killed in a mine disaster, his two surviving children immediately put the old orchard up for sale. Neither had lived in Tasmania for many years. Both preferred the clamour and glitz of mainland cities, and the warmth of cheap Southeast Asian resorts. Anything that kept them away from their family, their past, their strange uncle. Neither invited the idea of the country bumpkin made good and denied the presence of anything that wasn't normal. In their world being average was good and they both spent every minute of the day striving for normality.

The property was snapped up by a young family seeking their own normal, in the shape of green pastures and trees and above all a safe idyllic environment to bring up their children.

Cuddy was soon trailing his old push bike along Cherrystone Lane to the highway: a green racer, with cow horn handlebars, that he kept in the third room. It had previously belonged to his brother and came to Cuddy when his brother learned to drive and soon went to work in the mines on the mainland. He never gave it to Cuddy. He never gave anything to Cuddy but his name, but Cuddy always saw his brother riding it and waved madly to him without response.

A plastic bag, red, white, and blue stripes, fat and stuffed full, was perched on the saddle, flopping down either side. Through the gaping mouth of a busted zip, it threatens to billow clothes and towels across and along the road. At the highway, Cuddy takes a right and continues south. There are another seventy odd kilometres before the road runs into the Southern Ocean, at the end of the world, and far fewer villages and towns.

A few months later, as the main house was reroofed and the picker's huts boarded up, word filtered along the Lane, that Cuddy has found shelter at an RSL caravan park, where he was given a mildewed van, beneath an ancient crack willow, in the corner of the site, in exchange for mowing the lawns, taking the bins out and cleaning the toilet block.

On Friday nights he sits at the corner of the bar and is given a schnitzel and chips with a schooner of beer. While he eats, he reads the numbers that pass along the electronic ribbon of the keno machine but never buys a ticket. Later he cheers at the television as grown men fight over a ball. The others at the bar, in their tribal jumpers and beanies, don't understand Cuddy for he has no allegiance to blue, blue and white, red, red and white, red and black, red, white and blue, black and white, or any other colour or combination. He just likes the jumping and kicking and catching and cheers along. Most of all Cuddy likes the men in white coats and copies their gesticulations at every opportunity.

'That's just Cuddy,' explains the barman to visitors, across sodden bar mats and schooners of cold frothy beer, 'he's a bit soft, but a good bloke.'

Toward the end of the match Cuddy is waving his arms wildly as a shrunken old man in blue, from the far end of the bar waddles past, like a sick duck, heading for the toilet. He totters a bit, the beer he carries slops a bit.

The game is rabid with goals and as Cuddy winds up his arms to signal a score the shrunken old blue man totters back from the toilet colliding with Cuddy's sweeping arm. Beer spills, the glass smashes. Cuddy is shoved from his stool to the ground.

'Yer wee stupid fecker,' spits the shrunken blue man, 'yer owe me a beer, yer feckin halfwit.'

Regaining his feet, tension grows in Cuddy's limbs and his face flushes to a scarlet complexion. A tall man in black and white stripes, with moustache to match, looms over both men.

'Easy there old mate,' he attempts to calm the man in blue, by now rocking back and forth on his heels in Cuddy's face.

'I'll give you easy, the halfwit owes me a drink,' slurs the blue man and turns back glaring at Cuddy through two sunken beady eyes.

The barman, interjecting, passes over a beer, 'here's your beer Scotty, now leave him alone,' he orders, shaking his head, 'Who takes a beer to the dunny anyway.'

The blue man placated, offers no explanation and totters to the far end of the bar. The big man beckons Cuddy back to his stall and the barman plonks a full schooner in front of him. 'Here yer go Umpy, don't mind him, he's not from around here, he doesn't understand.'

Christmas Day

The rain squalled in from the west, dumped in the hills, drenched the Lane, and gathered to a froth in the rivulet by morning.

Baby Bear is the first awake on Christmas morning and runs to Mummy and Daddy Bear to cajole them awake, out of bed and into the living room to start Christmas.

'Mummy mummy the devils are gone.' huh-huh-huh, swallow huh. 'Did the rain wash them away?' Baby Bear's morning observation and relief overtakes her joy of Christmas Day.

'That may well be so,' says Mummy Bear, with a hug as cosy as a hand knitted jumper. 'You know Daddy Bear say's cleanliness is next to godliness'

'Where is your sister?' Ask's Mummy Bear. 'Go and get her so we can start Christmas.'

'I tried Mummy, but she won't get up.'

Daddy Bear calls out along the hallway, 'It's Christmas, come on Little Bear, it's present time.'

A mumbled incomprehensible reply bumbles along the hallway. Daddy Bear tries again. Another mumbled reply, this time approaching the door. There stands Little Bear in Christmas Pyjamas, hand over her mouth, tears welling.

Mummy Bear sits up in bed. 'What is it Little Bear?'

'I've been good Mummy,' she says with a snivel. 'I Really have.'

'I know you have my darling. Come to mummy.'

Little Bear takes two faltering steps to Mummy Bear, but stops short 'I don't want to be a devil,' she mumbles from behind a hand over here mouth.

'I can't hear you if you are mumbling my darling. Now take your hand away from your mouth.'

Little Bear takes another step toward her mother, burst into tears, drops her hand from her mouth, to reveal a front tooth, loose and hanging at an odd forward angle.

Upstream, beneath the tall pines, all is quiet. The two remaining women sleep long in their deep shade. Liz puts the kettle on. It whistles away while she decants away. Beth yells at her mum and rolls over.

'Merry Christmas to you too,' Liz yells back, hitching up yesterday's scruds and tracky dackies. For the first time she notices how she's changed what she wears, how often she changes what she wears, and feels she should have been exactly where she is now a granddaughter ago.

Back down the rivulet a low mechanical throb plays like heavy bass across the staccato sizzle of the fast rushing water.

Scary Pete, his beard not yet tamed to its three customary braids, silences his wife, and stretches on the verandah, taking in the chunky white foam riding on the surface of the churning creek. It puts him in mind of a freshly poured beer, the type he's seen a clip of from some sort of foreign beer festival, he watched on YouTube. So he cracks a tinny and cheers himself and his wives.

Where the torrent rips rocks and root from the rivulet bed Fiete stands his full height. Already stretched, he fondles his new niblick. He marvels at the rivulet that runs fast and runs past, his sandstone barricade. Satisfaction beams on his face, even as the white foam spews occasionally onto the top of his barrier, standing briefly firm. Brittle meringues on caramel squares.

He hunches slightly and chips a little white ball into a battered saucepan. It clanks and spins and spins. He listens to it settle, to its last gyration, then calls to his mother, in his mother's tongue, 'Merry Christmas,' and thanks her for his niblick.

It remains dark at the cabbage patch house but there seems to be a glimmer of light reflecting from the immaculately kept garden, as if the leaves of many greens themselves draw the light in and refract it through thick lenses of raindrops gathered in their wrinkles.

Wedgewood Cottage rests in a pall of gloom. If solemn has a tone that's how it sounds. Black spots multiplying in reach for the bathroom ceiling. Moss thrives undisturbed, spreading from the middle of the drive to blur with the lawn. Wallabies that once nibbled the grass close have died of kidney disease beneath the shady veranda, their shit and bones scattered along its length.

Yet further down the Lane, Linda and her five daughters and their partners sit around the big table, eating breakfast, while keeping watch over a swirling mob of children, that rush in and out and around the garden. No one sits at the end of the table and festive joy is muted, although all their restrained smiles are without blemish.

Memorial Park is a festival of tents and camper vans. There is little movement and only the rushing rivulet speaks, before a deep bark from a single black dog joins in.

Gradually the unwashed, those pitched in hollows first, a little damp, emerge to light stoves, make tea and coffee and fry things. Then attempt to find somewhere to dry damp sleeping bags.

I make coffee, pack a bong, and stare out at where my driveway used to be. Deep gullies, ruts and exposed rock will challenge even his driving skills. I sit in isolation scoffing the near silence, broken only by the rush of the rivulet and a distant, very distant, honk and hiss, that slowly seems to escalate to a chucking out time quarrel.

'I wonder if she found him?' I smirk, then cough and spew coffee and smoke.

Then the near silence of the valley is overcome and again I hope missing hiker, surely it was too early for much traffic to be on the road, too wet for fire and nobody works on Christmas Day.

But as the chop-chop-chop grows louder the machine comes into sight. It's not heading anywhere fast. Its mission this time to hover low above the orchard blow drying the fruit. So low I look down upon it as I look down upon my visitor's thinning and dimpled crown.

'Mummy mummy, it's Santa, he's come back,' yells Baby Bear, almost bursting her tiny lungs to achieve a volume to be heard over the noise, that bends all the trees in the garden and blows all the petals from the flowers.

Mummy and Daddy Bear order the children to stay inside and rush outside, where they stand beneath the blurring shadow of a helicopter that buzzes methodically around the house, then makes passes in straight lines that follow the regiment of trees.

Both look at each other, deeply puzzled, puzzlement sprouting fear and disappointment, then hurry back inside, where they tell the children again to stay inside, then tell them another fairy tale and promise them it will be gone soon.

Fiete waves his niblick angrily. He knows his mother will be upset. But also, that even his reach, coiled spring wind up and whiplash stroke is futile this time. On the shady bank across the lane cabbages tremble in the breeze and are deprived of their gloss.

Linda and her family ignore it in the knowledge it would be gone by lunchtime, or soon after, and get on with festivities, that this year include squabbles among the children and grandchildren over who will carve the goose and who will sit in Roy's chair.

While everyone else is arguing about the goose, two grandchildren, already tired of their presents, help Tinker into it. When they sort out the goose they turn to see and roar with joy born from loss that briefly silences the helicopter, in the knowledge that Roy and only Roy refused to have the dog on the furniture.

In the park tents billow and sleeping bags dry and take off and their tenants chase and work to peg and tie them more tightly, more securely, to the giving earth. Some look on with a smidgen of envy and desire at the campervans that sway gently as the chopper passes over.

It is well after midday before the glinting chrome and shiny red of the whirring bird departs. Perhaps the pilot too has a different type of bird to attend to.

The folk of the rivulet settle down to their lunch in the relieving quiet. Above the crackle of the rivulet the snap of crackers, the pop of wine corks, chink of glasses and wishes of warmth and goodwill trickle down the Lane.

Gradually the folk of the lane, bellies full to bursting, swap dining rooms for lounge rooms, hard chairs for easy chairs, cheer and goodwill for full belly groans and the desire to snooze, with or without an annually played movie, that they only see the beginning and end of but know so well they don't need to see the middle.

Scary Pete sleeps on his veranda, tinny by his side. Mummy and Daddy Bear snuggle on the couch, Little Bear close by. A sing-along cartoon plays in the cabbage patch house. Fiete rests his niblick and watches an ancient film with his mother. Wedgewood Cottage remains cheerless. Linda and the family take turns in minding the children. The sun shines and dries out the tents in the park, that seems oddly quiet and absent of activity. Then a scream punctuated by gulping sobs echoes up and down the rivulet.

'They're back, they're back. Mummy the devils are back,' cries Baby Bear. 'And they're all different colours this time,' chimes Little from behind a muting hand.

It was sometime later. After Little and Baby had been calmed with yet another fairy tale and others had been woken fully from their slumber and were picking over the carcass of lunch, that they really didn't need, that the Lane echoed to further alarm, alarm that seemed deeper, more widespread, than the squealing of two small girls. Alarm that seemed to be running in panicked scatter.

Soon the alarm, attracted different tones, different languages, greater noise. Wailing sirens, fast cars and an ambulance descended on the Lane. Police cars and emergency services turned into one of the tracks that led deep into the orchard, splashing more mud onto warning signs that read PRIVATE and DONT and DIE and something else that's mostly covered in mud.

Pickers of all shapes, sizes, and colours, gathered at Memorial Park, are counted, cordoned, and asked to remain where they are. Some forty odd pickers did as they were asked.

Blue and white tape, wrapped around and between trees, defines a wide no go area and a little sporty car, on the back of a truck, eventually emerges from the orchard, followed by an ambulance that is in no hurry, which is just as well as a column of fluffy bottomed geese need to be cleared from the Lane first.

He did make it up the drive in the new year and complained about the state of the driveway, then asked about Christmas Day. He doesn't usually mention that day, not for the last three years, since my own daughter said I was stoned and a bad influence on the children and turfed me out. She was right on the first part. But I think mostly she didn't like my presents.

If the girl has a wonky eye and twin rivers of snot to mouth that's what I see, that's what I paint. And if the boy is a tub of lard that can't keep his hands out of his pants, same thing. Doesn't mean I don't love 'em. I never lied to her and I'm not going start now.

I tell him I don't want to fix the drive, that I hope it will keep all those investigating the happenings of Christmas Day at arm's length.

He gazes along the Lane to the house that peeks out from beneath the looming pines that seems to wrap it in a shading thrall. Across the rivulet to the house in mourning and as the rivulet rushes to the old timber getters cottage that rumbles a couple of days a week with a mechanical roar. Then he comes to a house of grandeur and fairy tale repose.

Tracking the way the water flows he spies a thin man violently swinging a stick through the air before tickling softly a little ball into a cup. Across from which, perched on a shelf, a small home surrounded by green leaf sparkles as never before. Next door the paint is peeling from the cottage garlanded with the bones, the decay of disease and the gnawing and cry of feral cats.

As his gaze turns southward a tangle of kayaks rest on a lawn like a crazed game of pick up sticks. He looks across a vacant park, it's monument now clear of canvas hem, and onward over the flat expanse of the darkly shaded orchard to a distant figure trailing a pushbike laden with a gaping bag.

I pass him a coffee made pale. He clasps it in two hands lifts it to his mouth and speaks through the milky steam of all that he could see and says 'I hope what happened in the orchard was nothing to do with you.'

I sip at my own cup and proclaim my innocence, that 'I cannot see beneath the veil.'

'What do you think led her there?' He asks

'I understand she was on the trail of the owner of the birds that woke her up, that disturbed her idea of the peace and quiet of nature.'

'Do you think she found who she was looking for?'

'Probably not. I suspect nature is still clanging around beneath her perm.'

'Misadventure,' he summarises.

'I don't know. We were never formerly introduced.'

He glances up at me as I set down my empty cup and gather a small hammer that rests nearby. 'Now help me nail these pictures back on the wall.'

He swallows the last of his latte and follows me. 'Which one first?' He asks.

'You choose. It doesn't matter. We'll make a mosaic or a collage of my portraits.'

He passes me the man with motorcycles. I nail it onto the frame of the house. Then he lifts the one of the dodgy girl in the hoody, then the ordinary people.

Soon the bedroom walls are complete. 'Who knows if I get the house back together you might be allowed to bring the children for a visit.'

'Maybe old man, maybe.'

About the Author

Photograph of the author: Meng Koach.

David L Hume is the author of *Hidden Valley*, In Case of Emergency Press (ICOE), 2022, Melbourne. He has also published the chapbooks A *Tale of Two Holes*, a collection of poetry and the epic poem, *The Tragedy of the Little Black House* with the same publisher. His work also appears in anthologies and in online poetry collections.

David lives off grid and self sufficiently at the end of a small valley, along the Huon River in Tasmania, where he fishes and traps and grows lots of berries.

Formerly David has taught art history around the world, flirted with academia and published his PhD thesis as *Tourism Art and Souvenirs: The material Culture of Tourism* with Taylor Francis Routledge.

www.ingramcontent.com/pod-product-compliance
Lightning Source LLC
Chambersburg PA
CBHW051232210726
48290CB00003B/920